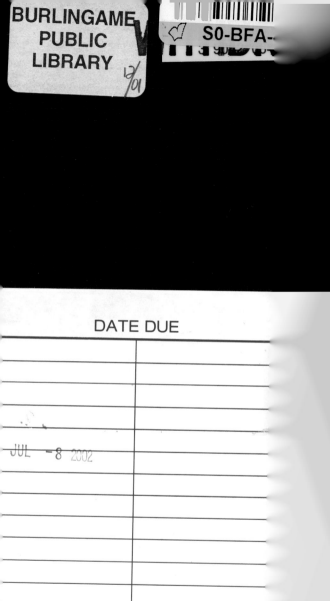

S0-BFA-

DATE DUE

BRODART   Cat. No. 23-221

A SELFISH WOMAN

A SELFISH WOMAN

Christopher Brookhouse

THE PERMANENT PRESS
SAG HARBOR, NY 11963

"Sunset" appears through the courtesy of *The Sewanee Review.*

Library of Congress Cataloging-in-Publication Data

Brookhouse, Christopher
    A Selfish Woman: a novel /by Christopher Brookhouse
      p. cm.
    ISBN 1-57962-036-1 (alk paper)
    1. Women college teachers--Fiction. 2. Cancer--Fiction.
    3. Middle-aged women--Fiction. 4. College students--
    Fiction. 5. Fathers--Death--Fiction. 6. Young men--Fiction.
    I. Title

    PS3552.R658 S45 2001
    813'.54--dc21   00-064247
                                                   CIP

THE PERMANENT PRESS
4170 Noyac Road
Sag Harbor, NY 11963

ONE

The river runs shallow. Dragonflies hover and dart above the silver water. Bees hum at the yellow centers of the asters. Fallen apples darken softly in the grass. Ironweed sways along the lane that ascends the hill to her house. She glories in the days, bares herself to the sun, walks undressed. I have no shame, she says to the light, to the dust, to the black snake stretched across the warm slate of the terrace. Well, almost none, for she can see anyone approaching the house, anyone driving up the lane, can quickly pull on her shirt and jeans. She loosens a tomato from its stem. She feels the buzz of pollen, the prickle of the tiny hairs of the vine. She bites into the warm, red flesh, juice trickling over her lips. She works her tongue into the crevices, pushing the fruit against her teeth, the juice running down her chin, down her throat, between her breasts, her new one and her old one. The new better than the old, her surgeon says.

Deer emerge in the bottomland on this side of the road along the river, browsing the stubble of the hay field. In the slant of light, the little farmhouse along the river, the one she rents to the visiting music professor, changes from white to rose, and she thinks she can hear him playing his piano. She hoped he might be interested in her. The day he signed the lease she wore a top revealing the tattoo on her shoulder, a tiny purple lyre. The man with his inks and needles and decorated all over like an islander she might meet in a Melville book had never heard of a lyre, other than the human kind. She showed him a picture. When he finished, he dabbed her skin with alcohol. You have easy skin to work with, he said. The surgeon had said the same thing.

She planned to invite the music professor to the house for drinks and supper, but she lost her nerve and was brusque and almost unfriendly until she learned to her relief that the man's companion was on his way west with the rest of their furniture.

Lights come on in the farmhouse and in the towers of the college on the hill on the other side of the river. Wearing a silk blouse, white, and a skirt, orange, the summer color of the fox whose den is in the bank by the locust trees, and silk as well, brushing her thighs, feeling like someone's breath on her skin, she strolls across the grass. She pauses to watch a car turn into the lane and begin to climb the hill and knows from the two yellow headlamps, one flickering on and off as the wheels bounce over the stones, that Julian Bristol in his ancient Beetle is paying her a visit.

The door slams. A tinny sound. She stands on the front steps. Julian wears a jacket over his white T-shirt, this department chair who idealizes James Dean, whose eyes glistened as he leaned forward attentive to the screen, the narrator's voice summing up Dean's thoughts just before his car collided with another on the gray California highway in the flat glare of late-afternoon sun. The other driver's name, spoken by the highway patrolman solemnly reading from his notes, was Donald Turnipseed. The students tried not to laugh. This generation has no soul, Julian said.

"Caroline, you're looking extremely well."

Julian kisses her cheek. His fingers drift across her back.

"Come inside, Julian, and have a glass of wine."

She holds open the door. He follows her into the kitchen. *"Danke,"* he says when she hands him a glass, his eyes scanning the room, scanning her blouse.

"It's my night for leftovers," she says, answering his curiosity about her tidy kitchen. Naomi, Julian's wife, is surely at home with her sleeves rolled up chopping and dicing.

He follows her again, into the living room to the couch. Their reflections and one of the lamp behind them appear on the glass, imposed on the hillside beyond. It reminds her of a playful perspective in an Altman movie.

"Cheers," Julian says. He tings the rim of his glass against hers. "Is that the house down the hill you didn't rent to Gerald Hanks?"

"What do you mean, 'didn't rent'?"

"I mean someone else, not Hanks, resides there."

"He didn't file a complaint, did he?"

"Does he have reason to?"

"Absolutely not. The remodeling wasn't finished. I told him if he waited a couple of weeks, I'd rent to him."

"I suppose you're so well off with rents you haven't given a thought to teaching again."

"Yes, Julian, I am, or think, or hope, I am well off. Rents have nothing to do with it. No one asked me to teach."

"Do you want to?"

"Not particularly."

Julian swallows more wine. "Hanks is sensitive, you know. People in Connecticut gave him all sorts of reasons not to rent to him. He doesn't understand how different we are out here. How much he's wanted."

"Wanted? 'Dead or alive'?"

"How much we need him. Better?"

"I'm sure he knows why."

"Filling our need for minority faculty isn't demeaning, not in my opinion. I hired him and I'm glad of it." Julian crosses his leg over his knee and tries to see out the window, past his own reflection and Caroline's. "I suppose the rumors have started already. Tell me what you've heard."

"Julian, if I did I'd be back in a person I don't want to be in anymore."

"I'm here to ask if you would join us again, Caroline. We're overenrolled in freshman comp and understaffed."

She bends forward as if hiding from Julian's words.

"Julian, I don't know. If you were offering the film course, that might be different."

"Caroline, are you bargaining with me?"

That time at his party, walking her to her car, asking her if she was all right to drive home, offering to take her himself. Naomi would want me to, he said, slipping his hand into her trousers, sliding his palm across her hip and breathing warmly against her cheek, that time he had offered her the film course.

"We've been down this road before."

"Interesting choice of words. I would have said 'up this road before'."

"Julian, you're not helping your cause."

Julian raises his hand, opens his fingers, a peace sign.

"Think about it. Two sections, no more than thirty students, I can offer you five thousand."

"All those papers, Julian."

"Five tops."

"It's not the money, Julian."

"I suppose Bob is paying you something."

"Bob doesn't pay me anything he doesn't want to or can't afford to."

"It's none of my business. By the way, how's Ellen?"

"She's working in Los Angeles. Doing well."

"I remember her fondly. Cheerful student."

"You liked the short skirts she wore."

"Of course I did. I'm not ashamed to admit it. See. Admire. Don't touch."

"Can we turn this conversation in a different direction?"

"Caroline, what are you going to do with yourself?"

"Besides continuing to get well, besides getting up every day and not having any plans except to delight in being alive?"

"All by yourself, up here on your hilltop."

"Julian, being by myself isn't a problem."

He sets his glass on the table. "Such a waste," he says.

His hand is warm. She takes pleasure from it.

"You mean I was a good teacher?"

"That's part of what I mean." He stands up. "Consider my offer, will you?"

"Julian . . . "

His finger presses against her lips. She can't remember the last time a man kissed her.

"I will," she says.

"And soon."

"How many sections does Hanks have?"

"One."

"Let him take one more."

"He's got two lit courses."

"I suppose you can't hire a minority and dump two comps on him."

"Not and keep him."

"I notice the film course isn't being offered this year."

"The department is debating it."

"Movies are too popular, I suppose?"

"Historically, we're a literature department. That's our mission. However, we may find a compromise."

"Are you bargaining with me now?"

"Caroline, I'm not here to bargain with you at all. I'm asking for your help. I hope you will give it."

Outside the crickets chorus. Moths fly to the light Caroline turns on for Julian to see to walk to his car. Eyes glitter in the grass. The tinny sound of the door again. Caroline watches the Beetle's taillights dim and disappear.

Another glass of wine. I should have told him about the book, she thinks. But she doesn't want the community to know what she's doing. A film book, someone will sneer. Really, a woman with a Ph.D. in literature more interested in popular entertainment. When Caroline mentioned starting a film course, her mother, dead now, remarked, You certainly have gone downhill.

Caroline looks out the window at the starry sky. Up the hill, Caroline says, remembering Julian bringing her home, his hand moving from the gearshift to her thigh. Caroline turns on some music and goes into the kitchen to warm leftovers in the microwave.

The night cools. Deer snort among the apple trees. An owl hoots nearby. The air is full of smells, the pungency of leaves and roots and loam. Even the rocks give off fragrance. She can smell iron. She can taste blood.

The town fills up again. New students with their families. Lines at the post office, the bank, the bookstore, where Caroline buys *The New York Times,* where she once sat staring at the cancer books in the women's section, sat too afraid to do more than contemplate the pale faces of the authors, read their bios, their survival stories, and wondered why should she consent, why she should not opt out of the cutting. There was comfort in knowing how one was going to die. She cannot reach down into those days of panic and despair anymore, cannot grasp precisely the calm moment of resignation when she chose to give in, when she buttoned her coat and drove herself to the hospital, where her doctor waited behind brick walls full of black winter windows. That's all behind her now.

She sits in an armchair by the bookstore window, the paper folded on her lap, and drinks coffee and watches the students consult maps and schedules, watches them follow the arrows pointing down the street to the academic building appropriately awash with light. Julian sees her and comes inside.

"Any decision?"

"Not yet."

"Look. One of the sections is the remedial course. I'll give you an assistant. It's mostly marking spelling and punctuation mistakes. The person I have in mind will do a good job. You can spend your energy on the regular students."

Julian leans toward the stack of Styrofoam cups on the coffee table. A card propped between the pot of decaf and the pot of regular says HONOR SYSTEM. There's a bowl to put money in.

"Whom do you have in mind?"

"Marion Marsh. Very qualified. Interested?"

Julian fills one of the cups with coffee.

"Could be. I should meet her first. Before I agree to anything."

"I'll arrange it."

"At the house."

Julian holds his coffee cup in one hand, the other searches his pockets for change.

"Name a time."

"One-ish."

"Done."

Julian kisses Caroline's cheek and scurries out the door without paying for his coffee. Caroline's hand follows the orange magic-marker squiggle that leads from the card to the bowel. She had followed the yellow line down the hospital corridor that led to oncology. Yellow, the color of daffodils and kitchens. Why not red or brown? Enough, she says. She drops two quarters into the bowl and goes outside into the blue air.

Marion Marsh. Caroline cannot remember a face, but something about the name sounds familiar.

Ten minutes in the grocery store, mostly checking the new videos. Slashers and peepers. Not for her. Home. 11:30. Caroline opens a V8. She pours the thick juice into a glass and carries it to the pool. Too early for the black snake. She wishes she had the courage to touch it. The slate is cool as a sheet under her feet. She drinks the juice, then stretches out on a towel on the cement above the water, the air scented with chlorine. She thinks of piles of clean laundry. A tiny plane drones overhead, silver and patient in the cloudless sky. The first drops of sweat dot her forehead. She pulls off her jeans and underpants, leaves her shirt on because today she feels less sure of herself than she did yesterday. In town so many strangers looked her over. The depth changes by inches. The water covers her knees, the hem of her shirt, her ribs.

Halfway back to the shallow end she notices the shadow. Her heart jumps. Even before she sees the man standing there she is pressed against the side of the pool where she can reach her towel.

"Exactly what do you want?"

"I'm sorry. Julian Bristol said you expected me around noon."

"You're Marion?"

"Gabriel Marion Marsh."

Caroline shakes her head. Why had she assumed Marion was a female? She bets Julian was counting on it. He'd enjoy seeing her cowering against the edge of the pool. Protecting herself from what?

"I can come back."

"Does Mr. Bristol always call you Marion?" she asks as she walks toward the steps at the end of the pool, keeping her back to him and pulling the towel across the cement. Two steps up. The water slides down her legs and soaks into the cement. She wraps the towel around her hips.

"People usually call me Gabe."

Caroline wishes he wasn't standing where she abandoned her jeans and underpants. She doesn't want him to touch her underpants with his eyes.

"This is awkward," she says. "I told Julian one o'clock."

"I can come back."

Caroline dislikes her girlish modesty before this man, this person, who is half her age. She bends her knees, scoops up her clothes.

"Wait here," she says. "I'll be dressed in a minute."

Inside the house she dries off, changes shirts, pulls on her jeans, pokes her feet into sandals.

Gabe has been watching the shapes of clouds reflected in the water. He looks up and takes Caroline in. Her gray shirt matches her eyes. Her hair is damp and parted in the middle. She pushes it behind her ears.

"Gabe, I haven't made up my mind to teach the sections Mr. Bristol offered."

"He told me that."

"What else did he tell you?"

A blush, just a hint of one; Caroline wonders if he's editing Julian's words.

"He said, Go up there and convince her."

That sounds about right.

"Okay. Convince me."

"I'm sure I can save you time by marking the remedial papers."

"Julian already thought of that."

"I can mark the regular essays too. The basic stuff. Punctuation, grammar, spelling."

"Computers correct the basic stuff. That's why the remedial students write their essays in class."

"I'm sure I can help you in some way."

"'Some way'?"

Gabe shrugs.

"I'm giving you a hard time, aren't I?"

"Julian warned me you would."

"Do you call him Julian to his face?"

"He asked me to."

"My daughter called him Julian. I thought it was because I did."

"Ellen?"

"Yes. Ellen. My daughter. Do you know her?"

"We're in the same class. I dropped out for a while. Now I'm making up a course to finish my degree."

"In English?"

"Studio arts. Photography."

"You dropped out to take pictures?"

"Not exactly."

Blond hair, a thin nose, full lips. He is handsome, in a way that makes Caroline uneasy.

"How well did you know Ellen?"

"We were friends."

Friends. Friends? Did you go out? Did you sleep together? Ridiculous questions, but they bob into

19

her mind like a row of ducks tracking through a shooting gallery.

"Ellen's working in California."

Gabe rolls up his sleeves. The pool is in full sun now. Caroline realizes she hasn't eaten. He follows her toward the house.

"Gabe, there's cheese if you want a sandwich. I've used up everything else."

"I'm fine," he says.

"Water or tea? I don't have coffee or sodas. It's too early to offer you wine."

Gabe asks for tea.

He sits at the birch table in the kitchen. Caroline's salad is already prepared in a glass bowl in the refrigerator. She whisks together oil and vinegar and pours them over the lettuce. She brews the tea and fills two mugs. She eats her salad and pulls bits of bread from a French loaf, dabbing each piece into a jar of honey.

"Do you think Julian slept with students?"

A question out of the blue. Caroline hopes Gabe doesn't think it's a mirror of her mind—or her soul, for that matter. Still, she's interested in the answer. She thinks of the page of rules recently added to the faculty handbook governing faculty and students. There didn't used to be any rules. Now untenured faculty risk dismissal; the tenured face censure and extra hours of committee work.

"You mean with Ellen?"

Caroline doesn't know herself if that's what she means.

"Gabe . . ." She takes a breath. Her tone softens. "Gabe, I was asking a general question."

Is it Ellen's life she's asking about or her own, the need to gather information she can use to get a favor when she needs one?

"I heard rumors about affairs with other faculty," Gabe says.

Affairs has an old-fashioned ring to it. In her own case, Caroline wouldn't call five minutes on the couch with Julian an affair.

She holds up her hand, as if pushing away Gabe's words. She clears her mind, returns to the choice she has to make.

"Gabe, let me confide in you. I'm at a place in my life where I need time to research and write. Teaching uses up too much time."

He is handsome. Could Julian be using him for bait? That's ridiculous, one more bobbing duck.

"You're saying no?"

"Almost."

"What can I do to change your mind?"

"Gabe, the papers are going to use up your time too."

"I work at the photo lab, but I need to earn more than that."

The holes in his jeans, the worn sleeves, his old pair of running shoes. Not a fashion statement then. Evidence of need.

"I've asked you a lot of questions, haven't I?"

"May I ask you one?"

At least he knows what verb to use. Julian probably didn't lie about his qualifications.

"As long as it's not personal."

"It is personal."

"Don't expect an answer."

"When I first met Ellen I thought she lived in Seattle."

"Her father does."

"Are you divorced?"

"Is that the question?"

"Part of it. Okay?"

"No, we're not divorced, and that's as much as I want to tell you."

"Would it be personal if I told you I used to see you at the college pool and you haven't changed?"

You mean, since they threw my breast away? How much does he know, Caroline wonders.

"Julian's plan isn't flattery, is it?"

"I meant what I said."

"Maybe I've changed in ways you can't see, but I appreciate the compliment, Gabe. I do."

Out the window Caroline notices the oil stain Julian's Beetle left on the asphalt. A rabbit hops over the grass, stopping to nibble, twitching its ears, alert for danger.

"Gabe, where's your car?"

"I walked. I don't have a car. I'm surprised Julian's managed the hill. It's steeper than I thought."

"You'll have to walk back."

"I expected to."

"Did you expect to convince me?"

"Not really. From what Julian said, I thought you would do what you want to do."

"Gabe, honestly I haven't made up my mind. But I will tomorrow. I can phone you or e-mail."

Gabe writes his number on a pad she uses for grocery lists. She walks him to the front door.

"If you want to know, Julian flirted with Ellen. That's all he did," Gabe says.

She stands by the window and watches him descend the hill, past the locust trees and the fox's den.

The sky clouds over. Darkness sets in. She imagines Ellen in California. Ellen works for a man who develops properties. Ellen reads proposals and treatments, sometimes scripts. Sometimes the man tells me to wash his car, Ellen says. She lives in an apartment above a garage. Caroline thinks of Kato Kaelin. Not a comforting thought. She decides to e-mail Ellen. Ellen came east for a few days after the operation, but she hasn't been back since. Bob sent Caroline a note wishing her a full recovery.

Dear Ellen . . . . Caroline tells her about Julian's offer and meeting Gabe. I know you remember him. Do you remember me? she wonders. Ellen has always been close to Bob. Bob told her over the phone from Seattle that Ellen supported his moving away, gave him encouragement. Just what a mother wants to hear. Tell me what you know about Gabe, Caroline writes.

Caroline returns to the pool. The underwater lights turn the water white. The air chills her skin. The water feels warm. She crouches down. Her breasts float on the water. They look nearly alike. We're getting better and better at this. You have to be a pro to tell the difference, the surgeon said. The air is clean and cold. Any malignant tissue, any renegade cells the surgeon missed cannot survive in such cold, pure air. She is sure of it.

Rain wakes her, a pattering on the leaves outside her bedroom window. She has always been a light sleeper. For hours she lay awake watching Bob sleep and wanting him. You're such a sensuous person, he said. He meant sensual. He was grateful for the way she made love. He preferred her to be the one who started things. Later on he said please don't; he had too much on his mind.

Caroline closes the window. The sky is pale. It's nearly dawn. She can see her way around the house. Ellen has returned her message. Gabe owes her fifty dollars. Tell him to pay up, Ellen has written, adding a comment about working hard and too much hot weather.

Caroline wonders why Ellen lent Gabe money and what he spent it on. Then she starts thinking again about Julian's offer. He needs her to teach two comp sections. He's offering Gabe to help her, to save her time. But Gabe's help won't save much. Then the idea comes to Caroline: With the money Julian pays her for two sections, and Gabe doing some of the correcting, she can hire him herself, pay him extra to search bibliographies or find the articles she needs and make copies of them, something that will really save her time.

She waits until nine to phone Gabe. He accepts her offer. At ten, dressed in linen trousers and wearing a black jacket over her blouse, a purple handkerchief pointing from the lapel pocket, she knocks on Julian's office door.

Julian peers between the books stacked on his desk. The walls are covered with framed photographs of Julian with famous commencement guests. His favorite is Paul Newman.

"Is Gabe acceptable?"

"You called him Marion."

"Did I?"

"Julian, no games, please."

"Do you know Gabe is Wheeling Marsh's son?"

"I didn't know. It didn't come up."

"What did?"

"My displeasure with Gabe arriving an hour early."

"I'm sure it was my fault. Mea culpa."

"I'm sure it was too."

Julian's eyes gaze at Caroline over the rims of his reading lenses. "Any decision?"

"Put the salary and conditions in writing and I'll sign."

Julian sets his glasses carefully on the stack of books. "I'm delighted you accept and sorry so little trust exists in our world anymore."

"I was married to a lawyer. Still am, in fact."

"Yes. Well . . ."

"I understand Gabe and Ellen were friends."

"She was, I believe, smitten with him. Quite a few young women are. He's very good-looking."

"I'm not too old to notice, Julian."

"That's why I sent him."

"Julian, I have no idea how far to take some of the things you say."

"Don't worry, Caroline. Haven't you heard? There's no meaning anymore. Everything's just text to be taken apart, just words that go in whatever direction anyone wants them to. I don't mean anything. Neither do you."

Down the hall she passes Gerald Hanks's open door. He's unpacking books, tenderly lining them on his shelves. She taps the frosted glass above his freshly minted nameplate.

"I'm glad you found a house," she says.

"I'm sure you are," Mr. Hanks replies.

"The timing was wrong. That's all."

"I met the people you chose. They're very pleased."

"Mr. Hanks, I didn't choose anyone."

"I know you believe that, Dr. Moore."

"Please. Call me Caroline."

"I'll do my best."

At the library Caroline asks to check out a video. "Can't," the woman behind the counter tells her.

"Can't?"

"Didn't you receive the notice?"

"I'm not on campus e-mail."

"Precisely the point. You didn't receive the message because you're not on the faculty this semester. Because you're not on the faculty this semester, you have no library status."

"Wait a minute. If a professor is on leave, she can't borrow a book?"

"You're an adjunct. That's different."

"Is this borrowing policy new?"

"Last spring it was decided."

"Who decided?"

"The library staff proposed the policy. Faculty approved it."

"Phone the English department. I am teaching this semester."

"Is your staff ID current?"

"No."

But my id's up-to-date. The voice in Caroline's head sounds like Groucho Marks. Caroline smiles to herself.

"You'll need to renew your ID before you borrow anything."

"What about renewing my ego?"

"Pardon me?"

"Never mind."

Blue dome of sky over the Gothic buildings. Her great-great-grandfather had been brought from England to cut stone for them. The ID office is in the print shop. A new magnetic strip is sealed over the old one on her plastic card. She's home by noon with her video. She fixes herself a sandwich of left-over chicken, carries her plate, the newspaper, and glass of juice outside. The black snake has shed its skin. Gray, translucent, oily to the touch, it goes limp in the heat of her hand. She leaves the skin under one of the apple trees.

Caroline has eaten half her sandwich. "Professor Moore?"

The voice behind her startles Caroline. The women are dressed in shorts and halters. Caroline knows Denise, not the other one. Almost all the faculty are addressed as Mr., Mrs., or Ms. *Professor* has an edge of sarcasm, as if there were quotation marks around it.

"Sorry. I thought you heard our car," Denise says.

"I guess I was concentrating." Caroline folds her newspaper and lays it down.

"Have you seen Gabe?"

"Not today."

"Someone told us Gabe walked up here. We were going to give him a ride."

The other girl is biting her lip.

"Denise, who told you Gabe was here?"

"Julian. I mean Mr. Bristol."

"Julian gets confused. Gabe was here yesterday."

"You must enjoy your pool," the other girl says.

"Professor Moore, this is Stephanie."

Caroline holds out her hand, but Stephanie is staring vacantly at the water. Caroline wonders if she's stoned.

"I'm real hot. Can I get wet?"

Stephanie is already slipping her straps off her shoulders.

"I suppose . . ."

Stephanie kicks off her sandals, pushes down her shorts. Caroline remembers a model wearing the same underwear in one of the *Vogue*s in the shop of the man who colors her hair. Sixty-dollar panties. Stephanie steps off the cement. The water widens. Bubbles wink with light. She comes up for air.

"Denise, how 'bout you?"

"If you don't mind," Denise says.

Denise jumps in. The girls laugh and splash each other, then stroke toward the steps, climb out, and rub their arms. Caroline decides not to offer towels. Denise and Stephanie sit on the warm cement, stretch out their legs, tilt their faces to the sun, and wait for the air to dry them.

"Are you okay now, Professor Moore?" Denise asks.

"I am, Denise. Thanks for asking."

"What was wrong with you?" Stephanie wants to know.

Denise frowns at her friend. "I told you."

"I had cancer," Caroline says.

"My aunt died of cancer," Stephanie says.

Denise rolls her eyes.

"Sorry, I shouldn't have mentioned it."

"Of course you should have," Caroline says.

"Thanks for the swim, Professor Moore."

Stephanie seems suddenly shy and puts on her clothes behind Caroline. In a couple of minutes the girls disappear around the corner of the house. The sun glints on their car going down the hill.

Where her father sent Caroline to school, the girls never appeared naked in front of each other. At night the sisters opened doors to find out if the girls were doing anything under the covers. The sisters oiled the hinges regularly. The doors opened without a sound. Now a woman near the college gives lessons on how to touch yourself. Caroline's friend Kay has described the women in a circle with vibrators. Some students petitioned to include the instruction in the women's studies curriculum.

Julian is the only man who has touched her since Bob left for Seattle. Now he fixes his attention on her chest, trying to determine from the crease of her shirt the way her body is changed under it. If he asked, she would tell him how one surgeon reconstructed her breast, re-created what another surgeon cut away. That night in her dreams Caroline watches Denise and Stephanie naked and giggling in each other's arms, arms long and flexible and quick as snakes; across the lawn a furious nun comes running, lashing the air in front of her with her beads.

"They have a crush on me," Gabe tells Caroline. "I'm sorry they bothered you."

Caroline has her class at ten. Gabe's phone is out of order. He's forgotten to pay the bill, he admits. She finds him in the photo lab in the art building arranging trays for the students, mixing developer and fixer, attending the row of enlargers, setting out panes of glass for contact prints, and tongs with different color tips to move prints from one tray to another. He is deliberate, meticulous.

"I have a set of papers for you to mark," she says.

Gabe opens a plastic bottle. The vinegar smell burns her throat. He switches on the safe lights. Her skin pales.

She walks up the path to her class. The borders are full of purple coneflowers. She has a doctor's appointment tomorrow. Some students say hello. She wishes they wouldn't notice her. Yesterday she wanted people to say how well she looks, today she wants to be invisible. In class she is scattered, takes long pauses. The students stare out the window, as if they can see her mind wandering under the maples. The cool evenings have tinged their leaves. The dragonflies have disappeared.

"Another day, another crisis," Julian says when she meets him outside Crowell House. "A leak in the pipes. Water in Hanks's office. Wouldn't you know. Maintenance has to rip down the ceiling. A real mess."

"He can share my office."

"Thanks, Caroline. I'll tell him. You look healthy, by the way."

She goes up the stairs to her office on the third floor and posts her hours on the door. There's one desk, a small bookcase, a set of file drawers, and a chair by the window. Hanks appears in the doorway.

"You heard about the misfortune?" he asks.

"These buildings are old."

"So is the White House, but one doesn't hear of pipes bursting over the president's head."

"His budget has more money for maintenance than ours."

"You have an answer for everything, Dr. Moore."

"Please use my desk. It's too early in the semester for my students to show up. I won't need to be here now."

"I applied for a carrel in the library, but there's a waiting list."

"That's not unusual."

"I could do my work at home, but I live far away and we have only one car. I can't come and go the way you do."

"At least the college has plenty of parking spaces."

"What is your point, Dr. Moore?"

"I wish you would call me Caroline."

At the restaurant Caroline and her friend Kay order salads.

"One group says you didn't rent to Hanks because he's black, and the other groups says it's because he's not black enough."

"Let's talk about what matters. Julian must feel he's qualified."

"Julian had to hire someone who isn't white. Mr. Hanks meets the requirement. A dozen others turned down the job. We're too isolated. No minority communities, especially no African-Americans, except for a historical fringe. No city close by."

"How many offers did Mr. Hanks have?"

"Let's say he needed a job. He's been asking about you too."

"How's my résumé?"

"Let's see. Ph.D. from a midwestern university. Publications: two articles, about film, so they don't count very much. Not tenured. Prefers adjunct status. Not a member of the Women's Caucus. Serves on no committees. Married. One daughter. Husband formerly college attorney, presently enjoying extended leave of absence. Health, B at least. Upgraded from D-minus. Rumored to have been close to department chair at an earlier time. The last information not verified."

"At least Julian doesn't brag."

"He knows how much Naomi will tolerate. She doesn't want to hear what she suspects."

Caroline watches a truck filled with soybeans pull off the road. The driver comes inside, sits at the counter, and orders pie.

"I'm going to see Pappas tomorrow."

"Should I worry?"

"It's just routine."

The county hospital is close to the college. Around it are fields, a wide road, barns, and silos. Dr. Pappas's nurse explains he has an emergency. The nurse takes Caroline's blood pressure and asks her to stand on the scales. Next she tightens a rubber tube around Caroline's arm. The needle slides in. Blood rises into in the cylinder. The doctor will phone, the nurse says.

The figure on the roadside, arm out, Gabe hitching a ride.

"Just in time. It's going to rain," he remarks.

He drops his backpack on the floor between his legs and fastens the seatbelt. "It's going to turn cold," he says. "I'm a sun person."

"I am too," Caroline says. "I have a list of articles for you to find and make copies of. Could you pick it up tomorrow in my office?"

"Sure," he says, slouching down as if he's angry with someone.

The wiper smears the first drops of rain across the glass.

"Gabe, I have no idea where you live."

"You can drop me at school."

"I have time to take you home."

They drive past the road to the college and loop around the quarry to the place where the river widens and a row of tiny houses and trailers is close to the shore. Years ago her father hunted ducks here. Some old cars and school buses have been abandoned among the trees by the water. Gabe rents one of the trailers. Caroline's car bottoms out in a wash in the gravel.

"Not much, is it?" Gabe says. "But it's cheap."

Caroline wonders about Denise and Stephanie. Too cramped, she imagines, for the three of them. Wonders where they go. Wonders if she's judging him, or them. Once Bob had commented that sex with two women was a common male fantasy. Lucky Gabe.

She turns off the wipers. Rain beats on the car. Too wet for the gray dog huddled under the sagging porch of the house next door to come into the road and bark. Caroline feels the chill and abiding dampness of this bottomland and of these rooms. There could be for her no recovery in this place so cheerless, so gloomy. Gabe notices the bandage on Caroline's arm. He reaches over and circles his fingers around her skin, his thumb under the bandage too beige to match anyone's flesh tone. He slides his fingers down her arm to her wrist. They linger as if exploring for her pulse.

He closes the door and goes up the cement steps to the trailer door and disappears inside.

The sky clears. Stars come out. A north wind. Protect tender vegetation, the weather voice warns. Caroline sits in front of the VCR taking notes on the film she's watching. Later, she finds herself hunched over trying to read the tiny letters of the credits, her pencil put aside, the fingers of one hand touching her wrist where Gabe had touched it. She can remember the sweat smell on his shirt, the scent on his skin of air before rain, the warmth of his fingers.

"Dr. Moore, do you know anything about the Defenders? I understand they operated here."

Hanks has taken over her desk, removing her papers and books to an empty file drawer. He points to a map of the county. He refers to the night riders who hunted down escaped slaves.

"My great-grandfather wrote about them in his journal."

"I'd like to read it."

"The journal is in the county history collection at the state archive."

"A photocopy would suit me."

"It's too fragile to copy."

"That's inconvenient."

"Some of the places he wrote about are still here."

"Perhaps you would be free one afternoon to show them to me."

"Let's wait until the weather warms up again," Caroline says.

Kay is almost on top of the Amish buggy before she pulls into the other lane and passes it. Caroline opens her eyes and wipes her palms on her jacket.

At the restaurant they sit again in a booth by the window. Across the street there's an abandoned house. The breeze blows a tattered curtain back and forth.

"I drove Gabe home the other day."

"I've been there. It's not much."

"When?"

"I went out with the deputy a few weeks ago. He had a warrant to search Gabe's trailer for marijuana. Of course he didn't find any. He got the warrant because he said a light for growing was on all the time. He just lied. He likes to harass the people who live there."

"I wouldn't like to live there."

"I'm told it's interesting sometimes. The men drink beer and rev their chain saws and dance around with them. Last year someone burned a cross."

"I hope Mr. Hanks doesn't hear about it."

"I spoke with him at a party. The way he talks, I can't believe he was born in Alabama."

"He's lived all sorts of places."

"The students are grumbling about him. He doesn't grade assignments and they don't know where they stand. Julian is going to have a chat."

"Probably no rule about grading each assignment."

"Honey, we have a rule about everything now. Old Bob would be moaning in lawyer ecstasy if he could read some of the stuff coming out of committees."

"I'm sure Mr. Hanks has his own system."

"I think he wants all the students to like him. He thinks being easy is the way to accomplish it."

"He's not succeeding with me."

"You don't count. Only professors vote in the review process."

"He doesn't get reviewed until the end of the year."

"Nothing like an early start."

"What's Julian's opinion?"

"Julian might tell you, but not me."

"I offered to drive Mr. Hanks around the countryside. Maybe we'll become friends."

"Don't ask for gas money."

"Gabe seems to need money."

"He's the son of a poet, what would you expect? I doubt his father sold more than a few thousand books in his lifetime."

"I forgot you wrote your dissertation on him."

"Honey, I got my job here because he recommended me. Wheeling Marsh happens to be one of a half-dozen worthwhile writers who ever attended our beloved institution. Julian is planning some sort of memorial reading of Marsh's work this semester."

"You'd think there'd be something in the man's estate to provide for Gabe."

"You would, wouldn't you?"

Morning starts clear and cold. Fog hovers above the river. The deer emerge from the water. Wisps of mist cling to their bodies. Their shoulders smoke in the light. Around the salt block the bucks duel each other. Their antlers sound like clashing sticks.

By noon the air is warm. Caroline sits by the pool grading essays. The car ascends the hill, the one Denise and Stephanie drove away in. Caroline is relieved to see Gabe walking across the yard. He has a towel under his arm. He hands her the pages of some of the articles she asked him to find.

"You could have left these in the office."

"Denise lent me her car to take pictures. She does that."

"Do you like her?"

"She's okay. She's generous sometimes."

"And unreserved."

"I heard. I'm wearing my suit. I hope you let me swim."

"The water's cold."

Gabe unties his shoes, pulls them off; unbuckles his trousers, pushes them down; pulls his shirt over his head. The shirt has a pocket. The boys she knew used to fill their pockets with packages of Camels. Gabe's trunks are green and baggy. He strokes through the water and the thin fabric clings to his hips. He stands in the shallow end wiping water from face.

"You're right. The water's cold."

Gabe dries himself in front of her. He slides his shirt over his chest. The band of his trunks has loosened in the water and they ride lower now. The curl of hair above the elastic is darker than she would have guessed. He wraps the towel around his waist.

"My husband left a sweater here that would fit you."

"Thanks, but I'll be warm in a minute."

Gabe sits on the cement near her feet.

"Is your husband coming back?"

"I don't think so."

"Do you want him to?"

"No."

Gabe turns around and faces the water. He rubs his legs with the towel. He has long thin feet, like his hands. She wonders if he ever played the piano. His blond hair sticks up in back.

"What did you take pictures of?"

"Mostly barns and silos."

"I'd like to see some of your work."

"I only have a few pictures I show people."

"May I see them sometime?"

"Sure."

He keeps looking at the water. She can't tell what he's thinking. His voice sounds unhappy.

"Gabe, are you all right?"

"I want to . . . I mean . . ."

"Gabe, what are you talking about?"

"I want to do something."

He's standing up now.

"Do what?"

He bends down, kisses her mouth. Her lips are still open in surprise when he moves away.

He picks up his clothes and walks toward the house.

You are a willful child. You always will be. His mother told him that. He was six or seven. He can't remember why she called him willful, what he had done to provoke her. Shortly afterward she moved back to England. Every week she wrote him letters full of advice, most of it directions on how to become an English gentleman.

Gabe did not disagree with his mother's assessment of his character then, nor does he dispute it now. He swings from thoughtfulness to acting heedlessly. Perhaps he inherited the trait from his father. Several of his father's early poems refer to reckless leaps from high bridges into the Ohio River or crazy plunges into the opaque water of abandoned quarries. When Gabe was sent home in the tenth grade for turning around and pushing his hand under the dress of the girl sitting behind him in the auditorium with her feet on the back of his seat, Gabe's father's only comment was, I did stuff like that too. The girl slapped Gabe's face hard enough to cut his cheek with the ring she wore, the stone inverted to make the band appear like a wedding ring. The scar is small, but it's there still.

Gabe meant the kiss to be gentle. He wanted her to like it. He wanted to leave things so she would want him to kiss her again. Yet he had no way of knowing what to do, what to say, how to act. So he had walked away and was now parking Denise's car in a student space behind the library, hoping Denise wouldn't appear and want to talk or do something else. He leaves the key under the seat and walks to the photo lab to empty the trays. Mostly, he's worried about tomorrow, being summoned to Caroline's office, being told he offended her. That she's not remotely interested in ever being touched by him again.

The figure model is leaving the building and waves at Gabe, the same woman whom he worked with in studio class, an angular body so pale and smooth it appears uninhabited. Gabe posed for the drawing classes his freshman year. The rules have changed. Students can't pose undressed for each other anymore. Both Denise and Stephanie have offered, but he has made excuses not to take their pictures.

Gabe drinks a beer in the Intimate, the tavern next to the barbershop behind the bookstore in the row of buildings the college rents to businesses. He decides to have another beer and order a pizza. It's almost dark when he leaves. He walks an hour before the man who runs the gas station recognizes him and stops his truck to give Gabe a ride home.

He finishes marking papers and reads for a while. The dog next door barks. A motor shuts off. Denise knocks.

"You left your notebook in the car." She hands him his book.

"If you leave too soon," Gabe says, "the deputy will think you're making a buy. But you'll have to go to the house down the row for that."

"You're what I came for," Denise says and takes off her clothes. She gets into Gabe's narrow bed.

His mind is far away, but his body is paying attention. Gabe's father wrote poems to his lovers. There were a quite a few. He refused to let doctors treat his prostate cancer. He didn't want to chance losing sexual function. He didn't lose it, not until the cancer spread.

"Professor Moore acted real surprised when we borrowed her pool."

Awake now, standing in her underwear by the counter, Denise is spreading peanut butter on a bagel. "Have you ever been swimming up there?"

"Once," Gabe says.

"When I was passing hors d'oeuvres at parties at the president's house, I used to hear gossip about her."

Gabe turns on his side and watches Denise suck peanut butter off her finger before she closes the jar.

"Your father's rich. Why did he tell you to get a job?"

"Daddy was in one of his snits. He said I spent too much money. He cut me off for a while. Want to know what I heard?"

Denise leans against the counter and chews the last piece of bagel. She moves her palm up and down between her breasts and her underwear.

"I heard she went free-range after her husband left."

"That sounds like wishful thinking. Someone who wanted to sleep with her and couldn't."

"You think she's attractive?"

"Yeah. Do you?"

"She seems kind of severe to me. Like prim, maybe. She said she had cancer. I think it makes her depressed."

Denise comes back to bed. "Can you do it again?"

Gabe takes longer this time. He loses interest, but he stays hard. Denise's mouth tastes like peanut butter. She trembles and raises her head and presses her teeth together. A sound like a growl vibrates in her throat. He wonders what sounds Caroline makes.

For nearly a week Caroline avoids seeing Gabe. She leaves a set of papers for him in her office. He returns them, graded, to the place on her filing cabinet where Mr. Hanks indicates he should stack them.

"I'm told you're the son of Wheeling Marsh. 'Wheeling' . . . what kind of a name is that?"

Mr. Hanks is growing a beard. A few curls of hair under his lower lip are white.

"'Wheeling' because he was born there. His name was Raymond."

"I know. I've studied your father. If you change his name around, he'd be Marsh Wheeling, a cigar. A rather strong-smelling, unpleasant cigar, let me add."

"He was aware of that."

"I'm sure."

It's not the conversation making Gabe uneasy, but the delay. He might encounter Caroline.

"You didn't have a conventional upbringing, did you?"

"I didn't have a mother very long."

"But women of some kind?"

"Most of them were nice."

"Do you know Marsh's poem that begins, 'Young and brown and bulging / With pride, into the oily channel / From the midnight span of the forbidden bridge, / We shouted farewells falling / Like lovely birds . . .'? What does *brown* refer to?"

Mr. Hanks glances over Gabe's shoulder. Gabe senses Caroline standing behind him.

"I suppose it refers to the skin of white kids who spend most of the summer outdoors without a shirt on."

"White kids. Precisely. And bulging? Sexual, would you say?"

47

"That's obvious from the rest of the poem."

"Do you think the poem's about race?"

"That hadn't occurred to me."

A hand touches Gabe's arm, guiding him away from Mr. Hanks's questions.

"Gabe and I have some things to discuss. Please excuse him."

Gabe follows Caroline down the steep staircase. They stand outside Crowell House under the blue sky. Caroline pulls a quince off the bush at the end of a bed of flowers, all brown stems from the first frost. She smells the yellowish skin and hands the fruit to him.

"Not exactly forbidden fruit, but it will do," she says. Her eyes are bright. She has brushed her lips with a shade of red that reminds him of carnations. He imagines it coming off on his mouth.

"Are you angry?"

"I never was, Gabe . . ."

"I've wanted to kiss you for a long time."

"Gabe . . ." Caroline is blushing, glancing around. No one near them. "Gabe, you can't be serious."

"My mother called me willful."

"Maybe she had a point."

"Tell me what you decided to tell me because I've been avoiding seeing you and I don't want to do that."

He holds the quince up to his face. The sweet

fruity smell makes his jaws ache. He walks beside her toward the parking lot.

Caroline leans against her car, its black paint hot from the sun, presses her skin against the metal, feels the heat through her skirt.

"You're staring at me, Gabe."

"You don't know how much I want to kiss you now."

"Gabe . . ."

"Don't worry."

Caroline's heart is pounding. What was she going to tell him? She can't remember, or she doesn't want to.

"Then you got in your car and drove away."

"You were waiting for me. I was late."

Kay is rearranging onion slices on her hamburger.

"What are you going to do?"

"Find a way to say no without hurting Gabe's feelings."

"That's what you're supposed to do."

"That's what you think I should do, isn't it?"

"Listen to us. We don't sound very sure of ourselves."

"Kay, I'm sure. For heaven's sake, he's Ellen's age. What would she think?"

"Caroline, Ellen's feelings aren't important here. Yours are."

Caroline bends across the table and whispers, "I would feel wrong about encouraging a man who slept with my daughter."

"Might have slept with your daughter."

"Which side are you arguing?"

"You said you drove away because I was waiting for you. You don't want to encourage someone Ellen was interested in. You're putting choices off on others. What do you feel? You, whose sex life since Bob headed into the sunset has been five minutes on the couch with Julian Bristol."

Caroline takes a deep breath. She has stored away the sensation of leaning against the car, the heat saturating her skin, working its way into her, arousing her.

"If we hadn't been standing in the parking lot, I would have let him kiss me. Okay?"

"Okay. Your feelings matter here."

"What should I do about them?"

"Remember your friend the circle lady. You can buy a vibrator and join up."

"Be serious."

"All right. There's all sorts of legislation about conduct of faculty and students. To be honest, it doesn't work very well. You can't legislate feelings. But you never heard me say so. I helped draft the legislation."

"What are you saying?"

"Listen to what I'm not saying."

The waitress pours Kay more coffee and leaves two checks by the squeeze bottle of ketchup in the middle of the table.

"What would you say if you were going to say something?"

"I'd say, Honey, have a fling. You deserve one."

It's Kay's turn to pay the checks. Caroline waits outside, a sky full of clouds, slashes of sun on the bare fields.

Kay closes the restaurant door. The reflection of a passing car speeds across the glass.

"I don't think I'm fling material. Anyway, why me? He's got Denise and Stephanie and who knows who else. What can I do that they can't?"

"You're making excuses again."

"Of course I am. I'm afraid. My body is more than twenty years older than his. For two years no one except my doctors have seen it. I'm not ready for someone his age to see it."

"Not it. You're talking about your breasts. Your breast. Gabe has seen the rest of you. Your butt doesn't sag. You don't have wrinkles or stretch marks or flabby legs. I've seen your breast and it's fine. Tell him. Show him. He won't run away."

"I'm sure he already knows. Who doesn't? Rumors are what we do best. Besides, you haven't touched my breast."

"Nice offer, but I'm not in the mood."

"You know what I mean."

"Caroline, what can I tell you? Be flattered. He's attracted to you. Chemistry isn't my strong subject. I take the stopper out and smell and if I like the perfume I wear it, and I don't bother to figure out how the molecules do what they do. See what happens. Your body is not going to frighten him away. That's what I wasn't saying before."

Standing on the side of the road, Caroline and Kay hug each other. The wind is blowing the curtain in the deserted house back and forth. Yes, Caroline tells herself, I would have let him kiss me.

Windy days. The pool man has treated the water with chemicals for the winter and unrolled the plastic cover. From time to time Caroline hears a shot. Men are hunting squirrels in the stand of hardwoods near the river. The scent of walnuts and hickories fills the air. Deer emerge only at night now. Pheasants gabble in the grass only early in the morning. Doves rest on the telephone wire, above the limp tomato vines, and mourn into the fading light.

The office door is closed. Mr. Hanks is gone for the rest of the day. Gabe unzips his camera bag and takes out a brown folder containing two more articles unloaded from Web sites he has accessed with the computers in the library. On hers, Caroline is composing a midterm exam for the remedial class.

"Let's go for a ride," Gabe says. "To take some pictures."

He sits in her car with the camera on his lap. They pass the quarry and fields and the deserted stone chapel and the graveyard where her family are buried. At the abandoned train bridge he asks her to stop.

The tracks have been taken up. Gabe and Caroline climb the weedy embankment. Sprayed on the rusty girders: Fuck, Peace, Kill; a cross, a noose, a dagger, a rose. Below, the river bubbles among black stones. The leaves from pale sycamores leaning along the shore float away in the frothy current. Gabe focuses on a heron standing near the bank. The shutter clicks. He refocuses and shoots again before he replaces the lens cap and stashes the camera in the camera bag left on the cinder roadbed.

She must know, he argues to himself. She must have considered before she drove away that taking pictures was not all he had in mind, must have known and must have said I will, I consent.

He touches her face with his fingertips. She closes her eyes. His lips are soft. He leans back, takes a deep breath, presses her to him. He kisses her again. Their lips are wet now. The tips of their tongues touch. She pulls away to breathe. She turns around, looks off at the river, the floating leaves, the heron in its thin shadow. His hands are under her sweater, his arms around her, pulling her into his warmth. She rests her cheek against his, feels the roughness of his whiskers, smells the air on his skin.

On the way home Caroline stops at an Amish store to buy bread and cheese. Farmers in the nearby field are cutting corn and bundling the stalks. The shocks resemble a row of tents against the fading light. A child in a bonnet and a long dress gathers pumpkins, lifting each one, arranging it among the others in the wooden wagon she then pulls behind her.

"You took only two pictures," Caroline says.

Gabe watches her heating soup to eat with the bread and cheese. The wine has a vanilla taste.

"Someone distracted me."

He raises her hair and kisses her neck. She likes having someone to talk to. She likes having someone to touch her. What was Kay's metaphor? The stopper is out of the bottle, but it's not too late to put it back.

She ladles the soup into pottery bowls, presents last Christmas from Ellen, sent with a note of regret for staying in Los Angeles to work over the holidays.

"I think Julian should ask you to read some of your father's poems."

"I wasn't planning to go to the reading."

Gabe is dainty with his soup spoon. Miss Manners would approve. He slices more cheese and offers the plate to her.

"Why not?"

"We're not on good terms. I'm still angry."

About money, she guesses. When she mentions it, Gabe shakes his head.

"He made me kill him."

Gabe stands and pours more wine.

"Gabe . . . ?"

"No, that's not true. He killed himself."

The cause was suicide, she remembers reading that in the obituary in *The New York Times*. The paper printed his picture, an old photograph. Their eyes, Gabe's and his father's, resemble each other, she thinks. The obituary included passages from several poems, and a list of lovers, referred to as companions.

"Julian is a great admirer of your father's work and he reads well. You might want to listen."

"Maybe I'll go," he says.

They take their wineglasses to the couch. Do you have a blanket or something, Julian had asked, already undressing, his tone slightly dismissive, as if she was incapable of foreseeing the need for one.

When she found one, Julian was already naked, his clothes piled on top of his shoes, ready for a quick getaway.

Gabe kneels and spreads her legs.

Kissing was one thing, but this . . .

He massages her calves, his palms pressing gently first, then harder, then gently again, gliding his hands higher until she feels his fingers graze the seam of her underwear. She bends over, concealing herself, her arms across her chest. He waits for a second, running his fingers through her hair. Let him, she thinks. Let him find out. Let him see.

She leans back. Gabe loosens her blouse from the waist of her skirt, unbuttons two buttons, puts his mouth on the skin under her navel, pinches a bit of skin between his lips, runs his tongue over it. He unbuttons another button. She draws in her breath. His mouth works up her skin. Then he stops and rests his cheek against her breast, the old one, and she knows he will undo all the buttons and place his hand on the cup of her bra over her new breast and touch it. Through the fabric at first, exploring the curve, lifting and stroking, approaching the aureole and the nipple, creations of her surgeon's skill.

She changes her mind, crosses her arms over her chest again.

"Gabe . . ."

Her skin tingles, its own set of memories awakening.

She thinks: yes, but not here with so much light, so many reflections.

"Gabe, let's go into the bedroom," Caroline says. On the way she stops in the bathroom and takes off her shirt and bra and puts on her shirt again.

Only a little light from the hall. She inches under the sheet. Gabe's hands upon her begin again, touching, unbuttoning, removing. She shivers. His mouth is warm. He takes the nipple between his lips, the one with feeling.

Now she must show him.

"Gabe, let me turn on the light."

She lies down again and puts her arm over her eyes. You are beautiful, he says. Then his arm is under her raising her up, holding her body against his, her arms around his neck. His neck is wet with her tears. She presses her legs together and turns on her side and finally goes to sleep in his arms.

Once she woke and thought she heard the tinkle of glass, the stopper from the bottle rolling away.

Indian summer. The campus empties for fall break. I have some free time, Dr. Moore. Would you give me the tour you promised? Mr. Hanks asks.

Gabe rides in the cramped backseat of Caroline's Toyota. Mr. Hanks is delighted to have someone along taking pictures. During the term his speech has sounded more and more like an imitation of an Indian accent. He explains he spent the most time in Bombay, but he's also lived in South America and in northern Africa. He's an expert in colonial writing and the writing of minorities.

"I'm a good hire. I should do well on my evaluations."

Caroline has heard his students are all making A's and B's, but they don't know why.

Mr. Hanks appears slightly sick as the car lifts and drops along the winding road. Caroline points to a brick cottage at the end of a lane of pines, where a man named Orion, the leader of the Defenders, lived. A collie barks and circles the car until a woman comes out of the house. She used to clean classrooms at the college and Caroline knows her. The woman holds the dog's collar while Gabe photographs the house and Mr. Hanks casts his eyes over it. Nothing remains inside from Orion's time, the woman assures Mr. Hanks. She points to the ground where the sheep pens were, where Orion once chained a slave who had escaped this far from Virginia and flogged him to death.

Later they stop at the Duffler farm, deserted now, the road dividing the house and outbuilding from the barns and tenant cabin. The roofs have fallen in. Soiled mattresses and feed sacks rot in the barn, the beams of the mow charred by fire. Pigeons flutter out of the hay door under the rusted tin.

"This used to be the Chase farm. Chase was a lawyer. The anti-Unionists met here. He was driven out after the war started. The Dufflers acquired the farm about 1870. Gradually, the family died out. The last one taught history in the county high school when I was growing up. He shot himself in the springhouse. Some bird hunters discovered the body."

"Didn't your father shoot himself?" Hanks asks.

"That's no secret," Gabe answers.

"Did you find the body?"

Caroline doesn't want to hear the answer. She starts walking toward the car.

Gabe says, "I found him. That's no secret either."

"I'm not implying that there are secrets," Mr. Hanks replies.

"There always are," Gabe answers.

Indian summer lingers. The basil in the kitchen window box revives. Gabe and Caroline wade in the river. The swollen papaws smell like ripe bananas. Red and yellow leaves scatter in bright air.

Gabe and Caroline lie in the grass. He caresses each breast. He kisses her scars. He tongues each nipple though he knows she can't feel one of them. There is no difference, he says, and though she does not believe him, his words please her. His hands, his tongue make her shiver. He puts his mouth where Bob would never put his. She gasps. Her hands grip Gabe's shoulders, squeeze and hold on until her trembling stops. She is too full and too empty to feel guilt or care whether Gabe is twenty or forty, or even what he has been to Ellen or she to him. He makes her cry out. Makes the world in front of her spin away. She loses focus, concentrates on only herself. Her body surprises her. She loses any sense of time. Distances fall together. Substances re-form themselves into essences. Sometimes he is earth, sometimes fire; sometimes she is air, sometimes water.

The students return. Kay comes home from Texas.

"Austin was a good place for a conference," Kay says. "Lots of beer, country music, flirting. Did I mention tattoo parlors? I was tempted. I suppose you spent the break doing virtuous things."

Caroline hears hardly anything Kay is saying. She's eaten half her sandwich and stared at Kay's mouth and thought about Gabe's.

"What did you say about temptation?"

"Nothing, really. I think that's your department. If Gabe has put that blank expression on your face, it becomes you."

The unfinished letter appears on Mr. Hanks'
computer screen:

DEAR LIBRARIAN,

MY COLLEAGUE DR. CAROLINE MOORE HAS
SPOKEN TO ME ABOUT A JOURNAL THAT CAME
FROM HER FAMILY THAT YOU HAVE STORED IN
YOUR ARCHIVES. SHE REQUESTS A PHOTOCOPY FOR
MY USE AS I AM RESEARCHING THE TIME PERIOD
COVERED BY THE DOCUMENT. CHARGE ANY FEE
FOR YOUR SERVICES TO ACCOUNT # . . .

Caroline supposes Mr. Hanks is downstairs
asking the secretary for the number. She gathers the
papers she came for and quickly leaves the building.

By suppertime Caroline isn't angry any longer,
only saddened by the lie the letter tells and the
mistakes in the telling. Her poor family, stored in
dusty archives!

Gabe is busy in the lab and with his own work.
Caroline misses him. After dinner she looks out the
window. On the road a car stops. She can't make out
more than its shape. Its lights go off. Soon they
come on again and the car speeds away. Sometimes
people let their animals loose, dogs and cats they
don't want.

Gabe closes the door. The trailer smells like pine soap.

"I brought you something from New York," Denise says. She unbuttons her coat. Her breasts fill the lacy top of her black teddy. "Want to see more?"

"I don't think it's a good idea tonight," Gabe answers.

"What would be a good idea tonight?"

"I need to work on my portfolio."

"Can I watch you?"

"That wouldn't be a good idea either."

"So, who is it, Gabe? Stephanie?"

"No."

"Okay, Gabe, but you're making a mistake."

Denise flicks her fingernails over the teddy. A nipple peaks underneath. "A big mistake."

After he hears her car drive way, Gabe unfolds the cloth he keeps the gun in. A Smith & Wesson .38. Short barrel. I don't trust Colts, his father said. He used to take the gun into the woods with him to shoot copperheads. They saw plenty, some thick and dark, some slender and pale. But his father never aimed at any of them, never pointed his gun, never fired at a snake. He was a good shot too. All but the last time, Gabe thinks. Snakes have as much right to live as we do, his father said, watching the tip of the tail disappear under leaves. Everything is holy, his father said.

"Do you believe he was right?"

Dr. Swenson is trying to quit smoking. He sucks an unlit cigar while he sits in a wooden armchair and listens to Gabe and takes notes. The office has no windows. A machine makes white noise on the other side of the door.

"He said writing was a holy act. Doing dishes was a holy act. Gardening. And most definitely fucking."

"But killing himself wasn't a holy act?"

"The point is, he didn't kill himself. I killed him."

Gabe shakes his head. What's the use? He's come to the same place before. Answered the same questions, but the anger won't go away. Words won't make it go away, his or anyone else's.

"Gabe, he was dying. Yes, he was alive, but he didn't want you to save him. He wanted you to wait. Wait. Let him die. If you dialed 911 the EMTs would have kept him alive. Gabe, you understand he didn't want that. He didn't want any more pain."

"He didn't want to live, but I had to kill him."

"No, Gabe. He undertook to do that himself. He didn't do a good job, that's all."

"I wanted to save him."

"He didn't want you to save him."

"Why should I care what he wanted?"

"Because the choice was his choice. Not yours."

"He made it mine."

"What did you expect to happen? You couldn't save him. No way. The man was riddled with cancer. Why keep him alive for another minute or hour or day? What would you accomplish?"

"Because there was a chance, just a chance, that he would see something, feel something, know something, understand something, that some revelation would come if he held on, if he endured the pain, if he just damn-the-fucking-pain held on."

"Gabe, he wanted to die. You didn't want him to. He cheated himself of a revelation, you think. He can't answer you now. Gabe, be gentle with him. Be gentle with yourself. Live your own life. Finish your degree. Take pictures. Fall in love."

Out into the gray air then, the cars going by on the highway thinning into the distance, the passengers ignoring him, the dry, cold air of deepening autumn cleansing his eyes.

The sky closes in. The first pale star appears. Up the hill at the end of the lane lights come on. Yes, everything is holy.

Caroline kisses him at the door. I was waiting for you, she says. The shower water beats against their skin. She has taken him into her mouth, but never this deep before, nor with such pleasure of her own, the different textures of his skin, its changing shapes on her tongue, its smell, its warmth. She can feel his blood beating. She has never wanted to do this with any man until now. She opens her palm, strokes him with her lifeline, her fingers lifting the pouch of skin underneath. Gabe cries out. He squeezes her fingers. His taste is tangy, warm, forbidden. She opens her mouth. Water rushes in.

They dry each other. Gabe squeaks a towel over the mirror above the sink. They pose. She in front. Head raised. His arm around her under her breasts. Her arm on his arm. Her other arm against his thigh, which is out of sight in the misting around the glass's edge.

The steep hill and the fear that someone could discover her, or that she would meet something in the dark, have taken Denise's breath away. Under the eve of the roof, crouched on hands and knees between the juniper and the wall of the house, Denise rises slowly until she can peer through the window. She sees, and leans away before the faces in the mirror see her.

Julian reminds the audience that Wheeling Marsh graduated with a combined degree in English and

French and attended graduate school on the West Coast before taking up the writing life full time, as well as accepting visiting lectureships at various colleges and universities.

Julian reads a short poem about kids drinking beer at night along the river. The students in the audience snicker. One of Julian's colleagues reads a poem about lovemaking in the backseat of an old Ford in the junk yard.

Kay and Caroline sit in the front row of folding chairs facing the lectern. Gabe sits off in the corner in an armchair, feet stretched out, arms folded across his chest. The audience is mostly students and faculty and a few wives and companions.

Several more faculty read. Julian concludes with "Sunset," a late poem written, he remarks, when Marsh rented a house in Florida before he knew how ill he was: "Here to this barrier island / We come, seniors in the slow / Thinning of ranks. We are leaving / This world no matter how we / Fill our days. So little shields us / From the other side of the sky. // Already snowing in the Greens. / Sleet subdues the prairies. Prayers / For the dead go out in muffled cities. / But here pines filagree the sky, / Cicadas shrill in leafy branches. / At night crickets cheep for love. // We bare ourselves to the sun, / Each bulge of greed, each / Wrinkle of envy. The young turn / Their eyes away. We are too naked / For their taste. They need tans / To take home, we need grace. // We settle down to the old / Reading, eyes on the vestments / Of the world; Earth Air / Fire Water. The alphabet washes up / At our feet, the tulip, the olive. / Variety. Order. We see. We are seen. // The red sun floats on the water. /Doors open. One by one / We gather on the beach. / We swim out of our wills. / Love surrounds us, / Forgiveness we do not deserve."

Julian invites comments. Gerald Hanks raises his hand.

"I'm concerned about the racist level of the poet's work. For example, the voice in the junkyard poem talks about his passion for the black woman he's with, how she fulfills him, although in physical fact quite the opposite is true, and how lost without her he would be. The physical act takes place in the backseat, but one can hear that word as 'black seat.' And where is this black seat? In a trashy old car, no good to anyone, except to strip for parts, exactly what the poet is doing. I'm sure the feminists will agree. The speaker's interested in one part only. It's like a photograph where the body's integrity is cut to pieces by focusing on only breasts or some other part. The act occurs on a nappy mohair seat. Where are we now but referencing the disparaging descriptions of older African-American men? And 'mohair.' A play on the disparaging dialect given

67

African-Americans—or worse, spoken by white impersonators, in entertainments for white audiences. Kingfish asks, What's that, Andy? Andy replies, That there's mohair. And Kingfish wipes his bald head and says, It's sure mo hair than I got."

Mr. Hanks waits for the laughter to subside.

"The poet is looking for this black girl to get him up. The poet is impotent. What does the poet see sticking out from under the front seat? The tip of a rod. A car jack. What is one of the common terms for masturbation? I needn't say it. Marsh's poetry is filled with references to rods and hard things. They're always around because the poet needs them. He doesn't possess their power himself. The irony here is this: The rod, the jack, is black. One could play around with the phrase 'black jack,' but the point is the poet is acknowledging white weakness, black superiority."

"Isn't that another racial stereotype?" asks someone behind Caroline.

Mr. Hanks smiles. "I know what my opinion is. What's yours?"

Caroline whispers to Kay, "He talks a lot better than he writes."

"Yes, but whose voice is he talking in? He sounds like all the articles he's ever read," Kay answers.

"At least he's a good reader," Caroline says.

A scatter of applause. The listeners stand up. Several faculty surround Mr. Hanks, appreciating him, listening as he goes on.

"He has a wonderful wit," Winston, the heir apparent to Julian's position, remarks to Caroline and Kay. "Not as much appreciated as he ought to be, don't you agree?"

Gabe leaves the room by a side door near his chair. What's he thinking? Caroline wonders.

"I noticed the Florida poem made Gabe a little uncomfortable," Winston says, "though I don't understand why it should."

Caroline and Julian stand on the path in front of the library. The clocks have been set back. The sky is unfamiliarly dark for early evening.

"What do you think?"

"I was interested in Gerald's remarks."

"I was interested too, but . . . I don't know. I suppose I'm losing touch. Winston feels Hanks is the hope of the department's future. He's certainly opened some eyes and won some admirers in the general faculty, especially among the science people who think we're spinning webs out of air anyway. Gerald's been nominated for a position on the faculty council."

"You hired him. If he succeeds you can't be disappointed."

"Tell me, Caroline, and this is none of my business, but did you ever think of suicide? Your cancer, I mean."

"No. I was depressed, but I thought things would be okay."

"What if you were in Marsh's place? Do you blame him?"

"I don't."

"Gabe does."

"I don't know him that well. He doesn't talk to me about his father."

"Do you know a student named Denise Dessen?"

"We've met."

"She came to me to complain about Gerald's teaching. I wonder how seriously to listen to her opinions. Her record is pretty mediocre. She says he never gives her any feedback. You're a good judge of these things."

"She's pushy. If she wants feedback, I bet she'll find a way to get it."

"I agree. I think she's used to having things her way. About Gerald, I want Gerald to succeed here. I really do. Do you know that Winston has invited Gerald to write an article on Marsh for the essay collection he's putting together?"

Caroline has the office to herself again. She's reading one of the film articles Gabe brought her, sitting in the comfortable chair by the window. The door is open. Cold air seeps around the window frame. She forgets how drafty the old buildings are. Men wearing jackets buzz across the grass with machines blowing leaves into piles. Denise's reflection clouds the window.

"I have some pictures I want you to give back to Gabe. You see him more than I do."

Denise lets the last comment linger in the air, a pregnant pause. Caroline remembers that drama is Denise's major. One by one Denise lays the pictures on top of each other on the table by the chair. "This was Gabe when I first met him." Gabe, his head shaved, wearing an earring.

"This was Gabe when he modeled for figure drawing." Naked, Gabe standing on a platform in the center of a semicircle of students straddling drawing horses, pads of newsprint propped in front of them.

Gabe reclines in cutoffs and a torn T-shirt, his eye squints through a gauze of smoke from the cigarette in his hand. Caroline wonders if it's tobacco. "Spring fling my freshman year," Denise says. "Same time," she says, and presses the last picture over the others. A sheet around them, Gabe and Denise. They appear to have nothing on under it.

Glare of a flashbulb in the mirror in someone's room.

Caroline assumes the effect of the tear shining in the corner of Denise's eye has been rehearsed, but she can't be sure. Caroline puts on her glasses and rearranges the pages on her lap.

"Gabe's not Gabe anymore," Denise says.

The sky is low and gray. Gabe wanted to borrow Caroline's car. She wants to be with him. She is driving. They follow a gravel road past an Amish school. Gabe loads his camera. The children are going home. Up ahead she can see the traffic on the bridge of the interstate. Gabe asks her to stop. She thinks he's going to shoot the picture, the girls in their long brown skirts blown by the wind, the boys in jackets and black trousers, these Amish children walking toward the bridge, the cars, the wake of diesel exhaust hanging in air that feels slick and toxic.

"Their parents wouldn't want me to do it," Gabe says, knowing what she's thinking. The children have their backs to him. In the wind they would never hear the shutter click, but Gabe puts away his camera. "Let's go," he says.

Gabe waves, the children wave back. Caroline drives in the direction of the quarry. The rain begins again, patters on the windows, dapples the surface of the water between the ledges below them.

Gabe pulls her to him, fills her mouth with kisses. She rests her head in his lap. His arms slide under her knees. He turns her around, her head against the door, her knees raised, his hands under her skirt, his fingers inching her underpants aside, unfolding the erect bud from its petals. The whole world is turning around, spinning on the tip of a finger and the tip of a tongue. The whole world is full of rain beating on glass, the smell of hair, the friction of skin. Nothing makes sense in this dazzle. Nothing matters in the circle tumbling from the center, the shuddering, the spiraling out, the release, the mind adrift in a drowsy wake.

That night Caroline gives Gabe the pictures Denise left in her office. Gabe tells Caroline about modeling, how the air always chilled him despite the heaters near the platform. In the first class some men smirked when he opened his robe, some women blushed and rearranged their drawing pads, fidgeted with their charcoals, tidying their space while their minds accommodated to the disorder created by his nakedness. He learned not to watch the class, but to gaze over it and think unrevealing thoughts. The money had been good. Too bad the college decided students shouldn't pose in front of each other anymore, Gabe says.

Had Ellen taken figure drawing? Caroline can't remember. Probably Ellen should have gone away to school, but the college offers free tuition to children of faculty and staff. So Ellen didn't go away. Caroline kept out of Ellen's life, gave her space, tried to make her feel she wasn't at home anymore.

"There's nothing in the rules about students posing for faculty, is there?"

"I'll ask Kay. She wrote the rule book."

"Ask her if faculty can pose for students."

"I think Kay would say the college doesn't encourage either situation."

"Then don't ask. Just let me take some pictures of you."

Caroline's mind swings from the honeymoon snapshots Bob took in Canada to close-ups of her breasts for her medical history.

"Let me think about it," Caroline says.

He tells her his teacher has hung some of his work in the department gallery.

Three messages on her machine.

"Mom, see you Thanksgiving."

Caroline replays the message, more surprised the second time.

Next, Dr. Pappas. Caroline's blood sample was inadvertently mislabeled, then misplaced, and now it's lost. Dr. Pappas apologizes. These things happen in the best of hospitals, he says. Please make another appointment.

Not until after Ellen's visit, Caroline decides.

Next, Gertrude Linden from the state library. She's received a letter from one of the college faculty. Ms. Linden objects to photocopying fragile documents. She is troubled by the writer's style and wonders if he exaggerated his position at the college. Does Caroline give permission for the copy or refuse it? Ms. Linden came to America from Germany. She is abrupt sometimes. Caroline convinces herself it would be unfair to deny Mr. Hanks's request.

Orson Mann teaches physics. He is Ms. Linden's brother-in-law. He stops Caroline walking toward the art department.

"I thought you people had computers that correct grammar."

"The students do. The department's equipment is out-of-date."

"Of course, I assumed no one in your area would need that sort of thing."

He doesn't mention the letter, but Caroline is sure that's what he's talking about.

"Sometimes we don't take as much care with letters as we should," Caroline says.

Mann smiles and walks away.

There are three black-and-white photographs signed G. MARSH at the bottom edge of the white mats they're mounted on.

An Air Stream parked along the river. The trailer glows in the light falling through the trees. The face of an old man with lank hair and a look of loneliness appears in the trailer's window.

Four shirtless boys in jeans sit on rocks at the quarry on a summer afternoon. Each boy is about fifteen. They have thin, smooth chests. Their ribs are showing. Each boy is smoking a cigarette. Two have them in their mouths, two hold them between their fingers. The faces betray little feeling except boredom, or self-absorption perhaps. Caroline thinks they must be friends with Gabe to let him take their pictures this way.

A woman lies on a picnic table, on her side, her legs tucked toward her chest, her face almost hidden in the bend of her arm, one eye fixed at the viewer. Around her, mostly out of focus, knives and forks.

Caroline is on her way with the midterm papers to Gabe's trailer. The November moon pales the fields. Lights turned off, she sits in her car above the river. The buzz and whine of motors fill the air. She sees Gabe hunched on the steps of his trailer. Among barrels of burning trash, men holding chain saws in front of them glide round and round lifting their saws up and down, felling invisible trees in the smoke, then turning to each other, waving the tracks of whirring teeth back and forth at one another's throats. She thinks of surgeons in gowns of smoke wielding their scalpels in arcs against the air and then sitting down to pick apart the woman waiting slyly on the table amid the clutter of knives and forks.

Caroline starts her car and backs up the road. At home she takes off her clothes. They smell like smoke from the fires. She stands in the shower under the beating water until the cold goes away and she stops shivering.

I BELIEVE THE POEMS OF WHEELING MARSH CONCEAL A SUBTEXT OF RACISM WORTHY OF CONSIDERATION AND THAT HIS WORK IS MORE REPRESENTATIVE OF DISCOLORATIVE TENDENCIES THAN THE WORKS OF NEARLY ANY OTHER POET OF HIS GENERATION. THEREFORE IT IS A PLEASURE TO ACCEPT YOUR INVITATION TO SUBMIT AN ESSAY ON MARSH TO THE COLLECTION YOU ARE PUTTING TOGETHER. COMPARED TO OTHERS I AM SURE THIS GATHERING WILL REFLECT MY PENETRATION OF THE LYRIC SHELL OBSCURING MARSH'S HIDDEN OBSESSIONS AND HIS ENDLESS NEED TO TAME THE

RUMORS OF IMPOTENCE THAT MUST CERTAINLY BE FOREGROUNDED IN HIM KILLING HIMSELF WITH A HANDGUN (PHALLUS) IN A MANNER HARDLY DIFFERENT THAN THE DEATH MADE FAMOUS BY MR. HEMINGWAY. I HOPE TO HAVE MY ESSAY IN YOUR HANDS BY THE BEGINNING OF THE WINTER SEMESTER. YOUR COLLEAGUE, GERALD HANKS.

"Kay, who gave you this?" Julian asks.

"Let's say a concerned friend did."

"Let's say someone who doesn't like Hanks's approach to Marsh's work. This doesn't impugn Hanks's scholarship. It's something dashed-off, although the quality is about as dismal as most of the babble published in our field these days. And the grammatical slipups are mistakes many of us make."

"Are you aware that students make up refer-ences for their papers because he never checks their sources? He never checks anything. Everyone's passing with flying colors."

"If a student brings a formal complaint to the review board, I'll hear it. I won't consider rumors."

"Julian, I find it hard to believe we can't hire a minority person who's better in the classroom."

"Mr. Hanks will find his way. He has excellent credentials."

"Julian kept the copy I showed him," Kay says.

"I hope he doesn't think I'm the friend who gave it to you," Caroline answers.

Kay taps sweetener into her tea. A dusting of snow is blowing across the roadway.

"Are we eating Thanksgiving dinner together?"

"My house. Ellen will be there."

"Really?"

"Downtime at work, she says."

"What do you say?"

"She's not coming at Christmas and feels guilty about missing two years in a row."

"At least she came back when you were sick. That's more than Bob could do."

"I never thought Bob would."

"For once Bob didn't let you down. Are you inviting Gabe?"

"I already have."

"I bet Ellen will be surprised."

"The other day I wondered if Ellen took the drawing class Gabe posed in."

"What was really on your mind?"

"How long do flings last?"

"When you get tired of the sex."

"Or he does."

"How are you going to explain Gabe to Ellen?"

"Spending Thanksgiving alone in a trailer doesn't seem right to me."

"That has the ring of truth."

"It is true."

"As far as it goes."

"Don't ask. Don't tell."

"Works for me."

Works for me, Caroline recalls in the jumble of thoughts she tries to make sense of. Nothing makes sense except Gabe's touch, his fingers stroking her lips. The flames in the fireplace heat her skin. Oil from Gabe's fingers infuses the air with the scent of sandalwood. Oh yes, it works for me. Oh yes.

Gabe straddles her hips. He warms more oil in his palms and smears it over her breasts. She knows her body is sweetly deceiving her, but she feels both nipples trigger currents that pulse and throb down the circuits of her body.

He sits beside her, smiling. "I like making you excited," he says.

Ellen arrives, driving a Cherokee she rented at the airport. I don't want to get stranded, she tells Caroline. Ellen swings the strap of the black leather bag over her shoulder and goes into the house.

Talking to Ellen is easier in the kitchen. It's Caroline's space. Ellen rearranges the apples in the bowl in the center of the table while Caroline fills the spinner with greens and listens to Ellen describe her work. Ellen refills their wineglasses with a cabernet she brought from Napa. Ellen's hair is brown, the color Caroline's used to be, with red highlights, darker than the wine, that shine under the kitchen light.

"Who's coming tomorrow?" Ellen asks.

"Kay and Gabe Marsh," Caroline answers.

"Mother, how thoughtful of you to invite him," Ellen says.

"It was thoughtful of Julian to suggest that Gabe help me this semester."

"Has he pulled himself together? Gabe, I mean."

"He seems okay to me."

"I bet he's still seeing his shrink."

Caroline doesn't comment, but she remembers Gabe thumbing a ride on the road near the hospital.

"He used to sleep with the gun under his pillow, the one his father shot himself with. I made sure the barrel wasn't pointed toward me."

Caroline doesn't want to hear Ellen talk about sleeping with Gabe. But her remark doesn't necessarily indicate they were in bed together, or what they were doing in bed. There's still room for doubt. But so little room that Caroline can barely persuade herself it exists at all.

"Gabe says he killed his father. I'm not talking shrink stuff here. Literally killed him. But he didn't."

Caroline sits down to listen. Ellen has an excited look.

"Wheeling Marsh shot himself, I know that much," Caroline says.

"Right, but he didn't do a very good job. Gabe came downstairs and his father was sitting on the library floor. If Gabe had called 911 the medics could have stopped the bleeding and tried to keep his father alive."

"My God, what did Gabe do?"

"He walked around the room."

"How long?"

"An hour, he told me."

Caroline tries to comprehend how anyone could do that.

"Gabe described the room. It's dark at that time of day. The air is full of river smells. There were books scattered on the floor and a fern in a brass pot that got knocked over. Later the house burned down. The police suspected Gabe of setting the fire for the insurance. But the premiums hadn't been paid. Gabe didn't get anything. Gabe says one of his father's lovers set the fire."

"Gabe walked around the room for an hour?"

"He knew his father didn't want to live. He had cancer everywhere."

Ellen slides her fingers up and down the stem of her wineglass.

"What about you, Mom? Your checkups okay?"

"They're okay. Thanks for asking."

"I'm dying to see Gabe."

Ellen regrets her choice of words. Caroline kisses her warm cheek and fills their wineglasses.

"Did you take figure drawing?"

"Gabe was one of our models. The other was Susie something. She had big hands and feet. Gabe was just about perfect. Great pecs. He used to do lots of weights. And he had those blue, blue eyes."

"He still has the eyes. I don't think he has much time for weights."

Ellen props her feet on the empty kitchen chair and watches her mother whisk oil and vinegar for the salad.

"So, Mom, are you seeing anybody?"

"Kay and I have a lunch date every week. I see Julian. Gabe, of course . . ."

Caroline feels her cheeks turning red.

"Come on, Mom, you know what I mean."

"Yes, but nothing serious."

"At least you're out there. That's great. I'm proud of you."

You wouldn't be if you knew.

"Does Gabe have a car?"

Caroline shakes her head. "Kay is bringing him."

Out the window Caroline sees the Cherokee and can guess the possibility Ellen is thinking about.

Wearing a long black overcoat, Gabe comes into the house carrying a casserole of sweet potatoes. Kay's special recipe. Caroline smells the nutmeg.

Ellen kisses Gabe's mouth. Kay sets a tray of rolls next to the potatoes and kisses Ellen's cheek.

"New coat?" Caroline asks.

"The coat was Ray's," Gabe says.

It takes Caroline a moment to remember Gabe's father's given name.

Ellen leads Gabe into the living room. They stand by the fireplace. Ellen keeps her arm around him.

Kay warms the potatoes. Caroline carves the turkey. It's nearly dark outside. There's so little daylight now. Caroline wonders if she should say a blessing at the table. She decides not to. She takes Kay's hand. "I'm thankful for you," she says. She and Kay stand for a minute in each other's arms.

Caroline brings the plates to the table. Wedgwood she received for a wedding gift. She doesn't care for the china, but Ellen does. When she marries, Caroline will give her the Wedgwood. Last night Ellen said she'd been dating a couple of men, a studio exec and a venture capitalist. (Caroline misheard and thought Ellen said "venture applest" and wondered what that was.) One has a collection of Porsches. The other collects Haitian primitives. Wedgwood probably isn't their style.

Ellen and Gabe are sitting on the same side of the table. From time to time she leans over and presses her shoulder against his or squeezes his hand. She's telling Kay about the work she does at the studio and some of the actors she's met. She doesn't mention the Porsche man or the capitalist. Caroline sees Ellen in a white veil. A crowd of people. Bob is there. Someone's immaculate lawn. Caroline sees palm trees and a limousine. Bob is with a blonde wearing a yellow dress that shows off her tanned breasts. She clings to his arm. Caroline can't see the groom. He's obscured by the guests.

Gabe says, "Ray used to invite a bunch of men to the house for Thanksgiving dinner. Guys who didn't have anywhere else to go. Ones he palled around with along the river."

Wheeling. A river town. Not glitzy California. Caroline imagines the room with the smell of the winter Ohio full of mud and oil and drowned animals, an old river house among the three-deckers peeling white paint. The porches sag one on top of another. The lawn chairs rust under the thin yellowish willow branches blown back and forth by the wind.

"Oh Gabe, you'll love this . . ."

Caroline has a hard time following the conversation, tunes in and out, avoids looking at Gabe, who, she realizes, is always looking at her as if apologizing. For what? The past? Or the future?

Caroline serves coffee and a pumpkin pie she bought at the Amish store. She opens the third bottle of wine. Ellen describes the wineries she's visited and the commercial the studio made at one of them in Napa. Ellen is holding a glass in the crowd shot. A split second at the end. You have to look hard to see her.

Caroline is relieved when Ellen stops talking.

"Let me clean up," Gabe says. Ellen offers to help.

Caroline and Kay sit on the couch with their glasses of wine. "Let's talk shop a minute," Kay says. "I did some checking on Gerald Hanks's credentials. According to Julian, Gerald has an Oxford master's. According to what I can figure out, Gerald enrolled in a program at a school called Finnesburg in northern England that allowed him to take some graduate courses at Oxford. Finnesburg is pretty much supported by its American enrollment and the master's it grants, and the transcripts it sends out emphasize the Oxford courses, not its own. It's pitch is that a Finnesburg degree is an Oxford degree. Which it isn't."

Caroline recognizes Kay's "give-me-some-advice" expression.

"If misrepresentation is involved, you don't know whether it's Julian's doing or Mr. Hanks's. If

Mr. Hanks turns out to be a good hire, the credential thing won't matter. Think of all the Harvard and Yale products who turn out to be duds."

"Mom, I'm driving Gabe home," Ellen calls from the hall.

Gabe stands in the doorway in his overcoat. "Thanks, Caroline. Thanks, Kay," he says. Caroline gives them a quick smile. She doesn't want to see Gabe and Ellen walk out the door together.

Caroline and Kay settle back. Car lights disappear down the lane. Caroline checks her watch. It's seven o'clock.

"Don't go yet," Caroline says.

"Good visit with Ellen?"

"Newsy. Not close."

Caroline walks around the room turning on lights.

"You're thinking about Ellen and Gabe, aren't you?"

"She changed when she saw him."

"I noticed."

"She's interested in two men in California. Both successful . . ."

"Say what's really on your mind."

"I almost think Gabe's the reason Ellen's here."

"Honey, be logical. Ellen didn't know you invited Gabe until she got here."

"You tell me what's on my mind then."

"You're involved with Gabe. You think you're a crummy mother. "

"That's part of it. Mostly I'm afraid, and it's my fault. I never imagined being involved with anyone like Gabe. I told myself to be happy with one or two friends. Live within myself. Take walks every day. Learn to love the winter as much as the other seasons. Stay well and survive. If I fell in love again, sexually in love again, I thought it would be with a woman."

"Have you ever been in love with a woman?"

"When I was fourteen I had a crush on Sister Frances. But Sister Frances loved Sister Hilda. The three of us were assigned to care for the school's farm animals. I'd find the sisters in the barn kissing. My father sent me to the school to keep me away from the raging hormones of the local boys. Watching Sister Frances and Sister Hilda wasn't what he had in mind. Gabe isn't what I had in mind."

"I don't think Ellen is what Gabe has in mind."

"Ellen can be persuasive."

"So can her mother."

"You're sweet, Kay."

"Of course I am. So what happened to the sisters?"

"Sister Frances and Sister Hilda left the order. They came to see me in college. They owned a kennel. They said I should visit. They weren't much older than I was. They said they wanted to spend more time with me, if I was interested in spending time with them."

"Were you?"

"No. I met Bob and started to date and gradually he filled in the blanks in my sexual education."

"But not completely."

"Kay, nothing could prepare me for what I'm doing. I'm sleeping with a man who slept with my daughter."

"You're sure about that? You asked?"

"Of course I didn't ask."

"Then you don't know, for sure."

"Kay, think about it. I should be waiting for Jerry Springer to call me."

"Caroline, think about it yourself. This isn't incest."

"It feels that way."

"Pleasure is moral."

"You can't mean all the time."

"I mean here and now. Just look at you. You're healing. You have a lover who's better for you than any doctor. And you're not hurting Ellen. It would be creepy if you and Ellen were sharing Gabe. Then Springer would call. Whatever happened between Gabe and Ellen is long past and over with. Nothing going to happen tonight. You'll see."

Eight o'clock. Kay says goodnight. Caroline reads for a while, then goes to bed.

She has a hard time finding a comfortable position. She has never had back pain before. Too much sex in different positions. Not a bad pain to have. She remembers she hasn't made an appointment with Pappas.

When the voice wakes her, Caroline gets up to make sure Ellen is all right. Ellen is pacing the living room and talking on the phone, asking about flights. "Yes, tomorrow, or today, I don't know what time it is . . ."

Eleven o'clock. Caroline could tell her, but she doesn't.

"Yes . . . good." Ellen presses the OFF button with her thumb. Caroline sees Ellen driving the freeways and talking on the phone, wheeling and dealing. She's Bob's child. Phones make Caroline uneasy. Too much bad news.

"Know what I think? I think Gabe's doing something with your friend Kay."

Ellen is pacing again.

"I think he's fucking Kay."

"Ellen . . ."

"Sorry about the language, Mom, but I don't care."

Caroline turns away to hide her smile. Kay was right. Ellen didn't get anywhere with Gabe. Caroline takes the rest of the wine from the refrigerator and fills two glasses. She unclenches Ellen's hand and presses a glass into her palm.

"Now, what makes you think Gabe and Kay are fucking?"

Ellen blinks, her train of thought derailed by the word she's never heard her mother say before. She laughs. Wine spills down the side of her glass. She licks up the drops with the tip of her tongue.

"Well, he's doing it with someone. I tried everything. He said it was someone older, someone I don't know."

"You know Kay."

"I think he meant, you know this person but you don't know that side of this person. And Kay brought him tonight."

"I asked her to."

"Maybe I'm wrong. I'm really pissed about striking out. Even the 'one for old time's sake' didn't work. Gabe's changed. He's like a hundred years old. Anyway, I need to get back to California. I'm on an early flight tomorrow."

In bed again, Caroline tries not to think how pissed Ellen would be if she really knew. Caroline is relieved that Ellen is leaving.

Dark by five. Twenty days until the solstice. A fine rain beads the windshield steamy from their breath and the heat from their skin. While she drove, Gabe's hand parted her coat, stroked her thighs. She pulled off the road and parked under walnut trees. Fields and a farm. A truck might come by, nothing else. Gabe works his fingers under the waistband of her slacks. She closes her eyes and leans her head against the seat and breathes deeply. This should have been the way it was thirty years ago, her mouth salty from French fries, being caressed by a boy in the passenger seat of his rusty Ford, her school-books scattered on the floor. Instead, she was saying prayers and tending the animals and pretending Sister Frances and Sister Hilda weren't rolling around in the straw. If she's silly to want adolescent sex, all hands and mouths, when she could be home in bed with Gabe, she accepts her silliness. Gabe delights in it, is filled with wonder when she gasps and presses her hand over his and squeezes her legs together. Then the silence, the pulling away. She opens her eyes and tries to put the world in focus. Gabe kisses her mouth softly. She closes her eyes again.

Gabe says, "You didn't see me."

TWO

ON the path Gabe had seen her, walking down the campus road from the classrooms to the gym, October noon, he on his way to the weight room and she, he guessed, to the pool, reserved at that hour for faculty swim. He left his backpack and wallet in one of the lockers, tucked the end of his T-shirt into his jeans, and decided to stop a minute to talk to his friend Dan, who sat in the lifeguard chair from eleven to one. Gabe inhaled the smell of chlorine and walked along a bright wall of tiles echoing the sound of swimmers stroking through the water.

Gabe saw her emerge from the women's locker room, tanned arms and legs, the gray one-piece suit riding up a bit. She hooked her thumbs under the fabric and tugged it down. She adjusted her bathing cap and dove into the jiggling water. He watched her swim on her back, watched the wet fabric reveal the shape of her breasts, watched the way her muscles changed shape under her skin. He forgot about weights and stood adoring this woman whose name he did not know, waiting for her to finish her laps, exchanging small talk with Dan, who sat hunched over on his tall chair twirling a whistle knotted to the end of a braid of string.

She ascended the ladder, not pulling herself up by her arms, but keeping her back straight, rising on her feet, her slender thighs shedding water. He watched her pull off her bathing cap, shake out her hair, dry her arms and legs. Before she disappeared into the locker room, she glanced up, saw him watching, and looked away, leaving with him the image of the moons of her hips as the door closed. Dan told him she taught in the English department. Her name was Mrs. Moore, Caroline or Connie or something like that.

Gabe desired her the moment she appeared from the locker room, desired to photograph her emerging from light, taking shape out of the tiles and mist of whiteness; he desired her the moment she regarded him and turned away.

He watched for her every day, timing his going to the gym to coincide with hers, following her on Tuesdays and Thursdays down the campus road, observing the way her body moved under her clothes, already seeing her atop the water, her breasts figuring themselves against the damp weave of her suit, water flowing over all her parts.

She's married to some lawyer, Dan told Gabe. Not bad for her age, is she? he added, grinning and swinging his whistle around his finger.

With a long lens Gabe photographed her, snatching images of her out of her privacy. He felt ashamed. He put the photographs in a box and seldom looked at them. He meant to throw them away, but she seemed too present even in pictures in a box to destroy them without causing her pain.

One picture was special, one of her in the pool. He had been taking photographs for the yearbook when he made that one. He held it back from the others he submitted to the editor at the end of the day's shooting and kept it for himself. He considered introducing himself to her. He imagined telling her his feelings. She would be polite, but she would be a faculty member and he would be a student. How could that context change? Anyway, there were plenty of girls interested in him, and he did not discourage them.

You might say I've been drawn to you, Ellen said to Gabe at a party, teasing with her eyes, hiding her smile with her hair.

Drawing class, he answered. I remember.

Then Ellen put her arm around him, as if claiming him for herself.

At dawn they drank beers on a porch and watched raccoons tip over a trash barrel and sniff through the scraps. He put his hand under her dress while he sat on the steps and she leaned against the railing. I'm sorry, he apologized, I'm drunk. So am I, she said. Her body pushed against his hand.

Gabe never knew her last name until they took a class together in the spring. He borrowed fifty dollars from her and brought her an expensive dinner when she came to stay with him at his father's house on her way back from Florida at the end of spring break. She met the last mistress, a gray-haired woman with wide shoulders, named Cherry. The name hardly suited her anymore. She had lived a hard life. Gabe caught her searching the house for money. She knew it wasn't in the bank. How could a writer like Wheeling Marsh be famous and not have any money?

Oh yes, his father said, writing is holy, fucking is holy, even washing your car is holy if you do it right and think about what God put into this world. Anything is holy if you consider what God put into this world.

So if God put you in this world, why are you doing this? Gabe said to the man on the floor. The blood from the wound in his throat soaked his shirt pockets, staining the denim a pinkish red that matched the color of the dust jacket of his last book, in which he had written, "Gabe, you are the only poem I care about."

Wheeling Marsh wanted to be cremated and to have his ashes scattered over the river. His lawyer advanced Gabe the money to hire the pilot and the plane, an old two-seater, open cockpits, the plane he flew people over the city in on Sundays in the summer. Gabe was nervous about flying and drank a few beers at a tavern with some of the men who came to the house at Thanksgiving.

Aloft, Gabe opened the box and flung a handful of ashes into the air. The air flung most of them back, peppering Gabe's face with hard bits of charred bone the size of pencil points. Gabe picked them off. Had Gabe wanted to look down as the plane banked over the river, he might have noticed the smoke. By the time the plane landed and Gabe had washed and driven home in the lawyer's car, the house had burned beyond saving and the firemen were letting it smolder to the ground. The next day strangers sifted through the cooling debris for valuables. Gabe let them keep what they found—a few pieces of flatware that weren't silver, but who could tell until the finders scoured off the soot; some vases that hadn't melted and might be a rare kind of glass; a beer stein with a goat head on the handle and German writing, which students at one of the colleges where Wheeling Marsh taught for a while presented to him. By the end of the week the lawyer informed Gabe that repaying the money his father owed the bank would use up most of his father's life insurance.

Gabe spent what was left on a ticket to upstate New York, where he enrolled in a famous photography course. In the fall, he returned to college and stayed in Ellen's bed for several nights, keeping the gun under his pillow.

He was sitting in the bookstore eating a bagel one morning with Ellen, waiting to hear from the dean about financial aid, when Ellen saw her mother passing by the window on her way to the post office. Ellen tapped on the glass and waved. Caroline waved back. Do you know her? Gabe asked. Of course I do. She's my mother, Ellen answered.

There were half a dozen students and faculty named Moore. Why would Gabe think one of those was Ellen's mother? Ellen had visited her father in Seattle and that's where Gabe assumed her mother lived as well.

Ellen went to class. Gabe went back to her room, packed his bag, and wrote a note saying the financial aid situation wasn't looking good and maybe finishing college wasn't important right now.

From time to time Gabe phoned Ellen, mostly to find out anything he could about her mother. When Ellen graduated, Gabe was living in Tennessee, waiting tables, taking a few pictures, renting darkroom space when he could afford it. Ellen was working in California when Gabe called and she told him her mother had cancer. Not like your father had cancer, Ellen said. My mother's going to be all right.

Even pain might be holy. What if a revelation had come to his father? What if on the threshold between worlds, his father wanted to return to this one to share that revelation, but Gabe had failed to summon help?

Death came in threes; chances came in twos. Maybe Caroline was going to be all right; maybe she wasn't.

Gabe ascended the hill to the house. He knocked on the door, called out "Mrs. Moore" through the screen. No answer. He walked around the house and saw Caroline in the pool in her shirt. The shirt was all she had on.

She frowned and turned and dragged the towel across the cement as she walked toward the steps. He could feel her anger and embarrassment. How gracefully she concealed herself and disappeared into the house and reappeared to invite him in. He sat watching her prepare her meal, admiring the neatness of the kitchen and her choice of jars and plates and bowls, imagining she was preparing a meal for them both and after they had finished she would stand beside his chair and he would embrace her and press his nose into the clean smell of her shirt and feel her skin rising and falling and her fingers caressing his scalp and the air would be full of no sounds except their breathing.

Not to be. Not now. Julian had sent him, Julian with his perverse humor. She had expected a woman, a woman named Marion. Marion, as in Marion Crane (Caroline, Gabe discovered, had written an article on *Psycho*.) Not Marion as in Marion Morrison, though *The Searchers* was one of her favorite movies. Gabe was the errand boy sent to deliver Julian's proposition and convince her to accept. He expected she would not, and she did not. That was all right because the context had changed. Although Gabe lacked one course to graduate, he was treated as if he had graduated. He wasn't a student anymore.

So he kissed her. Too surprised at first to object, Caroline held her lips against his just long enough to convince Gabe there was a chance.

Other kisses and embraces until he understood what she was afraid of and what was going to happen. The light was off. She approached the bed hesitantly. Bashful, she raised the corner of the sheet and inched into bed beside him and he put his arms around her and kissed her mouth. His fingers undid her buttons. No moon. No light. He parted her shirt. In short breaths she breathed.

He slid his hand up her chest. There. He had touched what she was hiding. Touched the most outer curve of its circumference. He opened his hand until her breast fit into his palm. She inhaled deeply, and again, determined, taking control of herself, until she stopped trembling. Gabe, she said, and did not finish; Gabe, let me turn on the light, she said.

She rose from the sheet and switched on the lamp by her bedside. She lay down again, her head on her pillow, her arm across her eyes. She seemed to hold her breath, as if the words he might speak or the thoughts he might think would hurt her. He kissed both her breasts, lingering on each only a moment, then pushed his arm under her back and raised her up and held her face against his chest. He whispered into her ear, you are beautiful. Her shoulders shook. Her arms circled his neck and she clung to him until the tears stopped. She turned on her side and he put his arms around her and did not move until he was sure she was asleep.

THREE

CAROLINE is on her way to the restaurant. She stops to adjust the seat. It's hard to find a comfortable position.

Noon. The sky is gray. Tiny bulbs strung around the restaurant window blink on and off. The waitress writes their order on her pad with a pen shaped like a candy cane.

Caroline tells Kay what Gabe told her, about the time he followed her to the pool. Kay doesn't seem surprised.

The waitress sets the plates on the table. She's wearing a copper bracelet.

"I've heard they work," Kay says.

"They do, if you have faith in them," the waitress says. She smiles and walks back to the counter.

"What were you going to tell me about Mr. Hanks?" Caroline asks.

"Gerald handed out course evaluations to his students. As required, he left the room while the students filled out the questionnaire. Instead of asking a student to take the material to the department office, Gerald collected it himself. Someone saw him culling through the responses. Apparently, he stuffed several into his pocket."

"I'm disappointed."

"But surprised?"

"He's under a lot of pressure, Kay."

"Really? I would guess the majority of faculty are on his side."

"Are you?"

"I'm uneasy about his credentials."

"Have you told Julian?"

"Not until I'm sure which way the wind is blowing. Incidentally, what's the word from Pappas?"

"I haven't gone yet. I'm sure I'm fine."

"I'm sure you are too. What about Christmas?"

"We just finished Thanksgiving. I haven't planned anything."

"Plan something with Gabe."

"Maybe he has plans."

"Caroline, he doesn't have any family. He doesn't have any money. Where's he going to go?"

"Maybe he's been invited somewhere."

"I know you're a Capricorn, but I wish you'd stop thinking like one. You and Gabe need to communicate."

"We do."

"On one level, for sure."

"Jealous?"

"Of course I am. Don't you think I'd like Gabe in my bed?"

"I never thought of that."

"I get tired being the shoulder to cry on for underappreciated, underperforming faculty males. We have so many of them."

"Does that include Julian?"

"I wondered if you'd ask."

"That's a yes?"

"I'm a survivor too."

Kay reaches across the table and squeezes Caroline's hand.

"Getting back to Mr. Hanks . . ."

"You're going to have to choose a side."

"I'm neutral."

"You can't be. You'll be contacted. Don't be surprised if Ross requests a meeting."

"Ross?"

"I told him my concerns about Gerald's credentials. He's the only person I confided in, except you."

Ross of the velvet touch, the president of the college, friend of Bob's. Caroline remembers Ross visiting her at the hospital, sitting on the edge of the bed stroking her arm with his antiseptic, pale fingers, promising her she would always be part of the college family as long as he was president.

"How's Julian going to react when he finds you went over his head?"

"Why do you think I slept with him? He needed assurance. I need insurance. He can't do much about it."

"Who's the captain of the side against Mr. Hanks?"

"Orson Mann, of course."

"What about in the department?"

"Higgins and Hoffman. The old guard. They were friends of Wheeling Marsh. They're very upset with Gerald."

"I don't like getting pulled into this."

"At least you can escape into the comfort of Gabe's arms."

How much Caroline would like that, especially on such a bleak December afternoon. For days Caroline has only glimpsed Gabe crossing the campus. Later today he presents his final portfolio to his professor. Gabe said they will probably go to the Intimate for a beer afterward. Caroline imagines Gabe's trailer. Those men with their blaring saws won't be there now.

"I'm late for the circle," Kay says.

"You're kidding."

"Just wanted to see if you were listening. You seemed tuned out."

"I was thinking about Gabe's trailer. I've never been inside it."

"You haven't missed anything."

"How did you get in?"

"The deputy was going to break the lock, but the woman next door has a key."

Caroline picks up both checks. "My treat," she says. The air outside has the damp feeling of snow.

Caroline drives down the rutted road and stops in front of Gabe's trailer. She picks her way among puddles and tries the trailer door. A neighbor stands on her steps and tells Caroline that Gabe's gone.

"Remember me?" Caroline asks. "I was here with the deputy that time you let us in."

The woman pulls her jacket closed and looks at Caroline. "I guess I do."

"Could you let me in again? I want to leave something. A present." Caroline points to the sack under her arm.

"You can leave it with me."

"That would spoil the surprise."

The woman laughs. "I'll tell you, I've let some others in with surprises, but those gals were a lot younger than you. You must have something special."

"I brought a bottle of wine to put in his refrigerator. He finishes school today."

"Maybe crazy Norman will play a song in honor of the occasion."

"Who?"

"I'll get the key. When you're inside, look out back and you'll see him."

The woman squishes through the mud in her rubber boots and opens the door. Caroline closes it behind her. She puts her face to the round window and watches the lady go home and remembers the man staring out of the window in Gabe's picture.

Gabe's trailer is about the same size. A table, a chair, a bureau, a bed, a closet, a bathroom, a tiny kitchen; a box of Wheaties on the counter, a jar of peanut butter, a plastic bowl and spoon in the sink, a pint of milk and a package of cheesespread in the refrigerator. Caroline lays the bottle of wine on its side beside the cheese.

In a box of books under the table Caroline finds a copy of *River Thoughts: Selected Poems of Wheeling Marsh*. The red dust jacket is the color of dawn. She opens the book. *Gabe, you are the only poem I care about: Love, Ray.*

Hanging in the closet she finds the overcoat Gabe wore at Thanksgiving. She wonders how it escaped the fire. There's also a leather jacket, a sport coat, a pair of dress trousers, a shirt, and a tie. She smells Gabe on the shirt.

On the closet floor she finds a stack of boxes that enlarging paper came in. She opens the top box. It is filled with prints and transparent sheets of negatives. The prints give off the chemical smell of fixer she remembers from the lab. She shuffles through several pictures before putting them back. Barns she recognizes, views along the river mostly in winter, sun glinting off the lacy fingers of ice, and a picture at the quarry of a shirtless boy sitting on a rock staring down at the ground between his feet.

She opens the bureau drawers. Underwear. Socks. Contraceptives in square blue pouches. A package of stale Camel filters. A page of instructions for a watch: German, French, Spanish, and English words too small for Caroline to read, and some in Japanese. The characters remind her of the feet of tiny birds.

Bufferin, toothpaste, toothbrush, a Tampax left on a shelf beside a roll of toilet paper.

Leaning on the shelf, two small prints fixed on mat board with clear tiny corners: another version of the woman on the picnic table, a rehearsal for the version Caroline has already seen; in this one the woman, Caroline is sure now it's a model hired by the art department, grins and gives the finger to the photographer, assuming he's the only one there. And . . . for a second Caroline does not recognize herself. To the other photograph she bends closer. She is backstroking in the roiled water of the college pool, her bathing cap sparking with the light, one arm reaching behind her, bubbles trailing in the shallow wake of her kicks.

The woman on the table; the woman in the water. Caroline studies the table woman again, her smile, her upraised finger; a woman lying among cutlery, a woman about to be devoured. Maybe she has the answer. Don't think about the future. It's the now that counts, the moment when you're whole, when the surgeon hasn't yet chosen his instrument.

Caroline turns on the kitchen tap and rises out a glass. While she drinks, she pushes open the tiny green curtain covering the window behind the sink. Down the hill toward the river a man sits on a folding chair, his fingers resting on the keys of a piano. The wood is warped and falling apart. The man wears a torn jacket and a felt hat. His face is tilted toward the sky.

Caroline again kneels by the boxes, opens each one, and fans through the contents. She finds more of herself. More of Moore. Too much . . . . Dozens of prints of her walking, sitting on a bench on a spring day reading the paper, talking to people, getting into a car, out of a car, standing on the sidelines at a soccer match, leaving the grocery store, the drug store, the bookstore, the library, the video store, the town hall. Adoration? Devotion? Obsession?

It occurs to Caroline that Kay has seen these pictures too.

"Dr. Moore?"

"Caroline."

"Caroline, may I have a word with you?"

Gerald Hanks closes the door, sits down, puts the pages on her desk.

"Caroline, this is the draft of my essay on Wheeling Marsh. I'm not a very good writer. To tell the truth, writing scares me. I wonder if you would read what I've written and mark where you think I should revise."

"You know I'm not very sympathetic to this piece."

"I know."

He crosses one leg over the other and tugs at the crease in his trousers.

"Gerald, what else?"

"I made a mistake. Now I need friends to support me. I don't know how many friends I have here."

"I think you know you have several enemies."

"I've heard you're not one of them. I thought you would be. I read the journal. I regret having requested a photocopy under false pretenses."

False pretenses. The phrase annoys Caroline.

"You lied," she says.

"I lied. But in a way I'm glad I did. Your family are interesting people. I'm unburdened by knowing about them."

"*Unburdened,* that's a nice word," Caroline says.

"I am. I found the names of some black families in the journal and I realize many of them are still living in the county. I want to learn more about their lives and how they survived. I suspect they have a history no one has asked them to tell before. I want to hear it and write it down. I'm sure it's important to know."

"I'm sure you're right."

"But first I need to survive myself, don't I?"

"I'm pleased you asked me to read your work, Gerald."

"I'm asking more than that. There's considerable pressure to put me out of here. Your friend Kay Michael, for example."

"If Julian stays in your corner, you'll be all right."

"Your friend has a lot of power. I've heard the president is grooming her for provost."

Caroline turns away to conceal her astonishment. For years the current provost has been on the verge of retiring. His wife wants to return to New England. Caroline knows that Julian covets the position. Kay has never mentioned it.

"Kay has the ability to serve the college well," Caroline manages to say.

"I shouldn't have mentioned her. She's your friend."

"Yes, you should. And I'm glad you did."

"Something off the record, okay?"

"There's nothing said here that's on the record."

"My Marsh article, it's just showing off, playing intellectual games, nothing I'm proud of. But without its publication, I'm doomed."

He stands up and gives a courtly bow. Caroline sees sorrow in his face. She wonders if he can see confusion in hers.

A car ascends the hill. The driver leaves Gabe at Caroline's door. He's a little drunk. He puts his arms around her.

He watches her undress. She feels him taking a picture. What does he see that she doesn't? It delights her and confuses her. She cannot see her face and her body the way he sees her face and her body. People never see each other without some sort of lens in the way, in Gabe's case the glass of wild exaggeration.

He makes her wet with his tongue. The world goes away. No Kay. No Julian. No Gerald.

When she wakes into it again, Gabe is standing by the window buttoning his shirt. Christmas lights glow on the tree in the yard of the farmhouse.

Gabe sits at the kitchen table while she cuts vegetables for stirfry. He tells her about his internship. He'll be on the road taking pictures three or four days a week for the magazine section. The paper pays for meals and a car.

"I was wondering if I could leave my stuff here. I don't have very much."

The oil in the skillet begins to smoke. Caroline keeps her back to Gabe. He means, leave himself here, move in, she thinks. The vegetables crackle. She lets them blacken before she turns them over and adds cubes of chicken. She switches on the fan. Its hum fills the room. Learn to love winter; keep things simple. Don't complicate your life, she tells herself. She can still feel his wetness inside her. What's so complicated about fucking? She blushes. That's Ellen's word. Is it heat from the stove that makes her warm all over? Or Gabe? Or the answer to her question?

She clicks off the fan. Silence again. She spoons rice onto the plates. Gabe opens a bottle of wine.

"When is your lease up?"

"End of the month."

"Gabe, let's decide later."

They eat and talk about films. She's surprised how many silents he's seen and remembers.

Gabe washes the dishes. Caroline dries them and puts them away. He tells her Kay wants him to do a portrait of her tomorrow.

While Gabe showers, Caroline sits in the kitchen in the dark thinking about Kay. Gabe will find the wine and ask the woman next door who brought it. That woman with the deputy, she'll tell him; and Gabe will thank Kay, and Kay will figure it out. And Kay will know Caroline has discovered the photographs inside the boxes.

When Caroline takes off her clothes, the bed is already warm with Gabe. She lies beside him and feels her skin soak up the warmth.

In the middle of the night the question works its way into her consciousness, keeps her awake: Was it

Julian's idea to offer Gabe as her assistant, or was it Kay's?

"Mind if I interrupt?"

President Ross fills the doorway. She always notices how well his suits fit him. He loosens his cashmere scarf and shakes her hand. The way he squeezes it before letting go reminds her of church: *Peace be with you, and also with you,* the priest making his way among the parishioners, shaking hands, the mask of sincerity flashed to each person there.

Caroline has almost finished reading Gerald's essay. The writing is better than she thought it would be. She's only had to mark a few sentences.

Ross closes the door and pulls a chair over to Caroline's desk. She feels crowded. The smell of Ross's aftershave reminds her of Bob's.

"You know, Caroline, a college president is like a politician. He spends most of his time fund-raising. He's the external president. The provost is the internal president. The provost keeps the college running smoothly, solves the hard problems. This has been an unusual semester for us. Smooth sailing, but the wind is picking up. I can feel it."

Caroline moves her fingers back and forth across Gerald's essay as if reading it in braille.

She wishes Ross would get to the point.

"Do you feel it?" Ross asks.

"Are we talking about Gerald Hanks?"

"Gerald. Yes. What's your read, Caroline?"

"You mean, whose side am I on?"

"It's come to that, hasn't it? Taking sides."

"I'm trying to stay neutral."

"Do you lean one way or the other?"

"Toward Gerald."

"Interesting. I understood he blamed you for his housing problem, then occupied your office for a while."

"We've had our differences."

"We need more minority faculty. No one disputes that. But I wonder if Gerald's our man. Furthermore, we have a prospect who's ready to come on board."

"Good."

"Good and bad. We don't have enough funds to compete for this man unless we free up one full-time position."

Caroline knows where Ross is going.

"You can't dismiss Gerald in the middle of the year," she says.

"If he misled us at the beginning, we could. In fact, we should."

"Bring on the lawyers."

"I think you're wrong, Caroline. If Gerald presented false credentials, he has no case."

"What if we, someone, misread them?"

"Then I'd say the person who did that would take the heat."

"You're referring to Julian."

"That shouldn't bother you. I assume you're sympathetic to Kay. Didn't you speak to the faculty about the need for more women on top?"

"I believe I said 'at the top'."

Ross rises elegantly from his chair and snugs the scarf around his neck. "Your words exactly. I'm glad we had this conversation. Keep an open mind, won't you? Don't lean so far in one direction that you fall overboard and the ship sails on without you."

Caroline sees Gerald returning from the registrar's office.

He says, "I've been saving this."

Gerald reaches into his jacket pocket and hands Caroline a folded piece of paper.

"I've heard the rumor I removed several evaluations. That's not true. Only this one."

The evaluations are anonymous. After EXPECTED GRADE the student has written A or B and checked "fair" evaluating the professor's tests and exams. Under COMMENTS the student added: "I learned nothing in this course. I should have taken Professor Moore's and found out how she gets her 'boy' to sleep with her instead of me."

"True, I read most of my evaluations first, before I turned them in. I was afraid of what they said about me. I recognized this student's handwriting. I didn't want anyone else to see what she wrote."

"I appreciate what you did. You're a friend, Gerald."

Caroline stops her car in the lane. The fields are brown and ready for snow, ready to wait fallow and frozen until the March rains warm them. That's what she is used to doing, hiding out until the snow thins and disappears and the tractors come forth under the wan spring sun to plow the fields and the cycle begins again. But Gabe loves photographing winter. He has nudged her appreciation of winter shapes, the fork of the bare branch, the shadings of gray on bark, the layerings of sky, the curl of grass, how the wind blows through it and darkens the surface of the river and moans in the beams of deserted barns. She moans too. Expressions of the deep pleasure of him inside her. Her body needs him. He makes her body feel whole. He is obsessed with her, but obsession is not love. He is obsessed with her body and obsessed with his father's dying. There is something he is not telling her, something about what happened that he hasn't told anyone; she is sure of it.

In her kitchen again Caroline brews herself a cup of tea. She thinks, It's you, Kay, you I should be in love with, who I am in love with as your friend, who I am so sad with. You used me when you needed to. I'll be all right. But Gerald won't be. It's Gerald you're going to hurt to get what you want.

Caroline walks about the house sipping her tea. The pictures, the pottery, the furniture, most of it she can keep and take with her, but the house won't be hers. She will lose it. Ross will be angry and tell Bob everything. The divorce will be handled by local lawyers in a conservative county. Bob will discredit her character before the judge. The judge will award Bob half the house. Money will be tight. She will have to sell her half. Friends will be hard to keep. Ellen may shun her for years.

By the time Caroline listens to the message that she missed her appointment, it's too late to phone Pappas's office and reschedule. She'll do it in the morning.

In the morning Kay phones. Ross has arranged for Kay to attend a conference of administrators, in Key West. I'm going down a couple of days before Christmas, Kay says. She asks when she and Caroline can get together to exchange gifts. How about a lunch before you leave? Caroline says. Wonderful, Kay says, as if nothing has happened.

Caroline phones Ross. She's leaning differently, she tells him. He invites her to his office for a chat.

On the way Caroline stops at the bookstore. In the gift section she buys an umbrella, one small enough to carry in a suitcase. When she went to Key West with Bob once, it rained for days.

"I'm pleased you've changed your mind," Ross says.

He gestures to one of the black wooden chairs decorated with the college seal and motto: ALQUID EX NIHLO ("something from nothing") and a man and woman (Adam and Eve, everyone jokes) under a tree sharing a book.

"Would you care for coffee?"

On a table with *Wall Street Journal*s are cups and spoons.

"Coffee is not on my diet," she says.

Ross looks concerned. "Yes, you must be careful what you drink," he says solicitously.

"I gave up coffee, but I drink wine. I'm probably not supposed to." She's sure he'll tell that to Bob. Evidence of irresponsibility.

"Now, how are you leaning, Caroline?"

"Away from Kay."

Ross strokes his chin and taps a pencil against the pad of paper by his arm on his desk.

"Weren't we considering Gerald?"

"We're considering Kay now."

"Kay's a great supporter of yours, you know."

"Perhaps we should cue the drumroll."

Ross shakes his head. "You've lost me," he says.

"Moments of self-destruction and all that . . ."

"Caroline, you're not making sense."

"See if this makes sense. If Kay tells Orson Mann and the others about Gerald's credentials, I will make clear that Kay not only knew about a sexual relationship that violates the faculty rules she helped to draw up but she also encouraged the relationship. Furthermore, in order to discredit Gerald further, Kay has spread the rumor that he removed several of the students' evaluations of his classes."

"You can't prove she did that."

"I can't, but I can start my own rumor."

"An adjunct with fangs. I liked you better in the hospital."

"Do you remember, you promised I would always have a place here."

"I was trying to do something for Bob. Any decision about you is up to the provost."

"I recommend you appoint Julian as acting provost and start a search for a permanent appointment. Let Julian be the internal candidate."

"Do you have any other advice, Caroline?"

"I've overstayed my welcome. I apologize."

"Apologies won't work this time, Caroline." Ross brushes his palms together. "Caroline, I'm sure you realize you're a selfish woman. You're hurting Kay. You're hurting the college. You're not doing Julian any favors."

"You left out someone."

"Who?"

"Me. I'm not doing myself any favors either."

Gabe brings her hot chocolate. She sits on the couch, her back against pillows, a blanket over her legs. Gabe stacks logs in the fireplace and lights the kindling under them. It's only four o'clock, but the air around the house is dark. Today is the shortest day of the year.

The bad news: Ross wasted little time. Bob phoned this morning. He had delayed the divorce to be sure she was completely healed and on her feet again. I'm not interested in supporting you or a lover, he said. Let's start the divorce ball rolling. Who's your attorney?

The good news: The renters in the farmhouse have bought a Steinway and the living room is too small for it. They've found a bigger house. They're moving in January. Will she excuse them from their lease? You bet, she says. At least she'll have a place to live when she needs it.

Now she's exhausted. She wants her mind to be empty. She wants Gabe to do what he's doing, sitting on the floor beside her, his hand under the blanket, massaging her legs, stroking her.

Later, she sits at the table while he cooks pasta and blends a sauce.

"I used to cook for Ray," he says.

"What about Cherry?"

"She thought famous writers hired cooks. She made rice and beans sometimes."

Gabe sets the table and pours the wine and fills the pot with water to boil for tea. She feels deeply exhausted. She always does at the end of a term. But now more than usual. She is happy, though. She presses her face into the wool of her sweater to hide her smile when she remembers how sweetly Gabe made love to her. They eat slowly. Gabe puts down his fork and holds her hand and stares into her eyes. She feels shy when he looks at her this way, as if he is reading her mind, perusing her secrets. There is one that says things are changing now, things are ending, a secret she tries to keep even from herself, but senses its presence the way one knows when someone else is nearby in the dark, has felt it hovering since she bent down and opened the boxes and found them filled with herself.

After supper Gabe and Caroline listen to music. She plays a Judy Collins recording, then some Sinatra. She's sure Gabe prefers something else, something closer to his generation, but he seems content and sits with his arm around her. The fire sputters and burns down. They go to bed and go to sleep.

Gabe has a car now, an Escort with a hundred thousand miles. The paper wants him to photograph some country churches for an article on keeping the faith.

Kay is already at the restaurant when Caroline parks outside.

Kay reaches across the table. Caroline's hands are cold.

"Here," Kay says, and gives Caroline a bright package. Caroline opens it and finds a pair of purple gloves.

"It rains a lot in Key West," Caroline says, as Kay unfolds the shiny paper around the umbrella.

"After you set the record straight, Ross changed his mind. No Key West. I'm going to Tucson to visit my brother."

"Sorry, Kay. I should have put myself in your place. I should have let you tell Ross yourself."

"You were me for a while, weren't you? Gabe thanked me for the wine. I didn't blow your cover. That lady has a terrible memory for faces."

"The idea of Gabe helping me was your idea, not Julian's, wasn't it?"

"Gabe's devoted to you."

"Obsessed."

"I prefer 'devoted'."

"You know what I'm thinking, don't you?"

"I know what you're thinking."

"Give me an answer. Please?"

"I meant to do you a favor. I knew how Gabe felt about you. I wanted to see what would happen. I wanted Gabe to make you happy. But what happened was Gerald Hanks. Julian should have checked Gerald's credentials better. Ross agreed. I saw my chance to court Ross's favor for the provost opening. I never though you'd do what you did."

"I had to defend Gerald. I'm sorry."

"Don't feel bad. You did me a favor. I need to explore other opportunities. Isn't that what one says in these circumstances?"

"I feel terrible."

"I could stay, honestly I could, but I've botched things as far as Ross is concerned, fouled the nest. He would never consider me for provost now."

"Oh, Kay, I don't want you to leave."

"Don't blame yourself. It's time for me to move on. It really is."

Caroline wipes her cheeks with her napkin.

"Honey, it was never personal. Not even about Gerald. I like him, but I think the school can do better. You disagree. Now he'll have time to prove himself."

An Amish buggy goes by the window, black horse framed against the snowy fields.

"I've never been to Arizona," Caroline says.

"Want to go with me?"

"I'd better stay here and start putting up with lawyers."

"Are you sure you're all right?"

"I'm sure," Caroline says.

Gabe and Doctor Swenson sit in his van. He fans smoke away from his eyes.

"I've given up trying to give up."

"Given up on me too?"

"As a patient, yes. You don't need me. But I enjoy it when you drop by."

"When Ray shot himself I was taking a nap. The noise woke me up. I think I was dreaming of him. I opened my eyes and whatever I saw in my dream fell apart into little pieces of light. Did I tell you this?"

"You told me you thought you were dreaming about one of your father's river friends. You thought he was keeping warm by a fire under a bridge."

"Now I think I was dreaming of my father."

"Under a bridge?"

"The window in the room where he died has a window curved like a bridge."

"And the fire?"

"Because Cherry threatened to burn down the house."

Swenson lights another cigarette from the one in his hand. "I'm with you. Keep going."

"My father thought his way into my dream. He was telling me he was about to die. I was always afraid of our house burning down. Lots of old houses like ours caught fire. I believed what Cherry said. The other thing is, he had told me he'd put in his will he wanted to be cremated. Fire again."

Swenson nods his head and exhales. "What else?" he asks.

"We had great Christmases. Ray's friends would come in and he'd play the piano and we'd sing all the songs we could remember. It wasn't the whiskey, Ray said, but the singing that changed the oxygen balance in our brains and sent us staggering around the room. Sometimes he would recite poetry, anything that came into his mind. Everyone listened. It was like Ray cast a spell. Everyone felt healed and beautiful."

White as chalk the sycamores by the river in the slant of sun. Long and dark the shadows. Caroline has her arm through Gabe's as they walk along the road. A rented truck is parked in front of the farm-house. Empty cartons are scattered on the porch. Many of the faculty have left for the holiday, but a few cars drive past. Won't be long before the word gets around. Tonight Gabe and Caroline are dining at the college inn. Her present to him. Why hide anything anymore? Why not go out in style? She smiles at the double meaning. Anyway, the change won't come again.

She wears a red dress cut low in front. She has never seen Gabe in a jacket and tie before. Gabe orders a whiskey. The server brings Caroline a wine. Gabe and Caroline touch glasses. The couple at the next table pretend not to notice. In the window beside her Caroline sees the reflection of the chairman of the history department and his wife observing them, as if Gabe and Caroline are specimens. Caroline leans across the table and presses her fingers to Gabe's mouth. He kisses her fingertips.

Another whiskey, more wine. The other diners eat quickly. Gabe and Caroline take their time, lingering over coffee and brandy. All evening Gabe's eyes have been on her dress and all over her body. Watching his excitement excites her. Is it because she knows things are ending that she wants him so much?

"I don't think I can wait to get home," she says.

"You don't have to," he says.

Gabe leaves the table for a minute. He returns, opens his palm, shows her the key. "I know someone who works here," he says.

In the hall she kisses him. He unlocks the door. The room is cold. They shed their clothes and pull the blanket over their shoulders. They kiss and caress. Their heat soaks into the sheets. Their smells come off on their fingers and mouths.

She cannot remember being this wet. At her age it's not supposed to happen. He glides back and forth, deep, then almost out, then deep again, then withdraws and kisses her some more and turns her over and slides in at a different angle. She grips the sheets, cries out. Drops of Gabe's sweat chill her back, adding to the bewilderment of sensations that all finally run together, and everything inside her swollen and tight lets loose, and all the nodes of pleasure connect and palpitate and shake the breath out of her, leaving her still and silent, uncoiling in languid transcendence, trembling every now and then from a wave so deep it has taken this long to curl and flutter up.

Christmas Eve. Pappas has agreed to see her.

"I have a present for you," Caroline says.

Pappas unwraps the brown shop paper. The photograph of the woman on the table.

"She's about to be devoured, consumed, isn't she?"

"I'm not sure," Pappas says, a bit confused by the gift and its meaning.

"I'm not either. The photographer needed money, so I bought the picture. I suppose I think of myself as that woman."

"And me as the devourer."

"Not you, the cells."

"Stand up a minute."

He presses on her bones.

"Pain?"

"Yes."

"A little swelling."

He presses some more.

"Caroline, I think we should do a bone scan. After Christmas."

The yellow line? The blue line? The green? Which will it be this time?

Although it is early afternoon, the lights on the trees in front of the hospital are on. Caroline's breath is white as smoke. Joseph is dressed in brown, Mary in blue. They stare at baby Jesus lying among bales of straw. The 4-H Club has placed wooden sheep around them. Across the fields snow begins to fall.

She remembers Pappas telling her before: a shower of cells, he said, making the ominous sound beautiful. She envisioned a bright display across the heavens, not invaders traveling in her blood.

Gabe has driven home with empty boxes from the grocery store and started to fill them with what he wants to keep. He's told the woman next door to take the rest. He uncorks the wine in the refrigerator and sorts through his pictures. He decides to burn most of them in one of the barrels outside.

He starts the fire with paper. It's snowing harder now. He feeds pictures into the fire. He's going to keep only one of Caroline, of her swimming in the pool. He wants to photograph her again. She doesn't want him to. Maybe she's changed her mind. He still has his key to the department studio. He's noticed she's lost weight. She seems moody lately. Distracted. Distant. She's changed since the autumn. She's a different woman now.

Gabe stands away from the heat. He sees Norman hunched over his piano. He's covered with snow, a luminous being, like a wraith created by digital effects.

When Norman walks toward the heat, the snow turns to water. His form, bundled in dark clothing, emerges. Gabe thinks he sees his father coming back, re-forming out of the bright pieces of dream light, fitting together again. Gabe is shaking.

"What's the matter, Gabe? Did I spook you?"

Norman pulls his coat out of Gabe's hand.

"Sorry," Gabe says.

Gabe gives Norman the wine bottle.

"What were you playing?"

"*Silent Night.*"

Wine dribbles down the corner of Norman's mouth.

"Stick around, Gabe. You don't look happy."

Caroline tells Gabe she's going to the midnight service at the college chapel. I'll go with you, Gabe says.

After dinner Gabe gets into the shower with Caroline, soaps her arms and legs, swirls the bar around her breasts, washes her hair. She watches their reflections in the mirror as he dries her. She discovers the delay between what she sees and what she feels. She watches herself watching.

Gabe kneels and kisses her. It is the season for spiritual adoration. All her adoration has been physical. She feels the breath of guilt. In the chapel she confesses and asks forgiveness.

Gabe sits with the prayer book on his lap. During the sermon, he leafs through Psalms. Then he closes the book and closes his eyes. He fidgets. This is not his place. He is uncomfortable here. When he opens his eyes, she feels the different way he looks at her. She is becoming real. When she takes communion at the altar, he does not go with her. She is going in one direction, he another. This is what she wants. This is what must happen.

ONE A.M.. The locks of the Escort are almost frozen. The air bites through their coats. Gabe works the door open. She sits shivering in the seat beside him. The sky has cleared. The heavens appear deep and black.

Gabe's boxes are stacked in the hall.

"Do you still have your father's gun?'

"In one of the boxes," Gabe says.

"Did you find the gun in the ashes?"

"The police had it."

Gabe reaches into his pocket and hands Caroline a present wrapped in silver paper. Inside she finds a prism of antique glass with a tiny wire to hang it from. She hooks the prism to the shade in the kitchen window. In the morning she holds out her hand. The visible spectrum vibrates in her palm.

All Christmas Day Gabe seems edgy. He sees me now for what I am, she thinks. The house is filled with her life. His life is in his boxes. He opens a map, locates the towns he plans to visit for the magazine, writes route numbers on a piece of paper, and tucks it into his camera bag.

"I want to take some pictures of you. Let's go to the studio," he says.

"Can't we do it here?"

Gabe sets about arranging lamps in the bedroom. He poses her in bed and by the window, checks and rechecks the light, adjusts and readjusts the tripod, decides on a different aperture, reads the light again.

"I can't get you right," he says.

You can't pose me in the past anymore, she thinks. You can't put me back into your imagination. I am not there anymore. Not inside you anymore.

"Let me do one of myself," Caroline says.

She puts on her tank top with the thin straps that reveals the lyre on her shoulder. She sits in a chair and bends forward, her arms across her breasts. Gabe releases the shutter.

He slips the straps down her arms. "Tell me what you like," he says.

She is not ashamed to tell him. One system of her body is betraying her; another has never been so perfect. Her mind turns off. No Ross. No Bob. No Pappas.

Gabe is photographing in one of the river towns in the southern part of the state. Kay is on her way to Tucson. Caroline sits by herself looking out the restaurant window. The waitress with the copper bracelet asks if the hamburger is cooked the way Caroline wants it. It's fine. I'm not very hungry, Caroline says. The restaurant is almost empty. A snowplow driver is drinking coffee at the counter. The cook wants to close up and go home.

Six months of chemotherapy, radiation after that, Pappas explained. You'll do fine, he said. You're strong.

At this moment it's Gabe's strength that she is thinking about.

Caroline comes home to Gabe's boxes, to what is in them and what is not. The book, the coat, the gun—Caroline's thoughts keep coming back to these things.

Gabe returns after dark. He senses Caroline in one of her moods.

"Gabe, why did you sleep with a gun under your pillow?"

"I was afraid of the dark," he tells her.

"Gabe?"

He taps the prism back and forth and stares out the window.

"In case Cherry found me."

"Why would she want to hurt you?"

"She was like that."

Perhaps she was. Caroline can't disagree.

Caroline picks up the pictures Gabe took of her on Christmas Day and spreads them out on the table, sets the one showing her tattoo in the center.

"You said the police had the gun, so the gun wasn't in the fire. Did the police have your camera too?"

Gabe blinks and hesitates.

"I took my camera with me."

"Took it up in the plane?"

"I left it in the car at the airport."

Caroline concedes this explanation too. Gabe takes a deep breath.

"What do you think of the pictures?" Caroline asks.

"Technically they're okay."

"But you don't like them?"

"They're not me. I'm copying other people's work. The tattoo one's the best. It's got a nice mood to it. But you set it up."

"Gabe, why don't you tell me the truth?"

"No. I can do better work."

"I'm not talking about the pictures. Your answers don't make sense."

"Why not?"

"Because you sit in a van in the hospital parking lot with your therapist."

"So what?"

"You keep coming back to him because you haven't told him the truth and you want to."

"We sit in the van because I'm not his patient anymore."

"That's my point."

"You don't make sense either."

"Why would Cherry burn down the house?"

"She wanted stuff and she didn't get anything."

"If she knew there wasn't anything to get, why bother?"

"She was angry with Ray."

"She knew long before he died she was going to leave empty-handed, but she stayed around."

"She didn't believe him."

"All the more reason for her not to burn down the house."

"You don't know Cherry."

"You're right, I don't know her, but I still don't think she did it."

"Do you think I did?"

"I think you started the fire and left the house and took what you wanted to keep, your camera and your father's coat, a signed book of his poems, you may have even had the gun, and by the time you were up in the plane the fire was out of control. By the time you landed, the house was gone."

"The house was the only thing of any value my father owned. Why wouldn't I want to keep the house? The house was my only inheritance."

"Gabe, I know your body, but I don't know your secrets."

"And you think you should?"

"For your sake, Gabe, someone should."

"Take your best shot."

Caroline considers Gabe's choice of words. Who is shooting whom? And with what?

"You didn't stay in the room with your father, did you?"

Gabe turns away from her, slaps his hands against his legs, then faces her again.

"Do you want me to describe the room to you? How it smelled? How the light changed? How Ray's pain sounded?"

"I'm sure you can tell me all those things. I think you spend a lot of time there."

"What are you saying?"

"I'm saying you didn't stay in the room. I'm saying you can't forgive yourself for not staying."

"You're saying I really killed him?"

"Of course not. That's what you say. That's what you tell people, so that they can tell you you're wrong. Admit it, Gabe. You didn't stay with your father, did you?"

He presses his sleeve against his face. Caroline puts her arms around him. She almost wishes she hadn't asked any question, almost.

Gabe pushes away, walks around the room, putting distance between them.

"The police had it right," he says. "I did set the fire. I wanted to burn everything. All the past. But it didn't work. Ray won't let go of me."

"Let go of him, Gabe. Let go of his death. Hold onto his life. Hold onto what he wrote. Hold onto his words. They're what matters."

Gabe slumps to the floor and sits among his boxes. The therapist must have told Gabe what she is telling him, but he wasn't listening before. Now he is.

"It's time for me to let go of you too, isn't it?"

"There's nothing to keep you here."

"You're here."

"I'm here and I'll be here if you need me."

"But you don't need me, not now."

"I do need you now, Gabe. I need you to be my friend."

Gabe's expression changes. Puzzlement, as if she has asked him a question and is waiting for the answer.

Finally Gabe looks up. His smile is boyish and charming and sad.

"I can do that," he says.

In the morning Gabe carries his boxes to his car. The air is dry and cold. Caroline holds Gabe in her arms one more time.

He pulls the door closed. She waves. His car descends the hill and disappears where the road curves along the river. She notices the way light moves over the apple branches and how the snow is sculpted away from the bottoms of the trees. Work of the wind, winter's psalm.

Jays shrill in the hemlocks. Chickadees flutter in the junipers. Deer tracks curve down the hill. The hillside sparkles in the sun.

Keep things simple, she says. Keep things simple.